CHRYSALLIA
THE PRINCESS of POSSIBILITY

A MODERN FAIRY TALE

ROBERT JOHN DE SENA

ISBN: 1491079711
ISBN 13: 9781491079713
Library of Congress Control Number: 2013913705
CreateSpace Independent Publishing Platform
North Charleston, South Carolina

Cover design by Dan Gottlieb

The image of Chrysallia on the cover was inspired by my niece Lindsey Hamlin. Like Chrysallia, may she slay her dragons and find her flower

CHAPTER 1:
A QUEEN IS MOURNED

The first contingent of mourners reached the coffin where Queen Beldonia lay in state. They draped it with wreaths of purple sarquella flowers that grew in the rich volcanic soil below the waterfall leading to the Forest of Fendor. The mist from the free falling water was rich in nutrients, and the sunlight that intruded through the rebounding droplets contributed to the unique beauty of these royal blooms. They were never disturbed except for the most sacred processionals in the Kingdom of Calderont.

Most public funerals in Calderont were celebrations because the formal belief system of the people embraced the notion of a continuation of the spirit beyond the visible form. That was not the case now. Anxiety, fear and rancor infected its good citizens due to the untimely death of their beautiful queen. Change had come to Calderont in the most unwelcome fashion and with it a doubt about the future that foreshadowed an impending decline in its culture.

From its very inception by the tribe of Calderi who emerged out of the gloom of the Forest of Maladour, Calderont enjoyed a unique history. Bounded by forbidding woodlands and a desert, the population enjoyed an evolving, dynamic civilization uninterrupted by war or invasion from their neighbors. In fact, not much was known about any surrounding kingdoms. As long as could be remembered, no one ventured past the forest thresholds, and no one had ever emerged from any alien origin through these secure boundaries. Armies were unnecessary in such circumstances, and given the rich bounty of vegetation, animals, and natural fuel sources, the good people of Calderont forged an impressive culture. Men and women were treated equally, and both played pivotal roles in raising their children. Expressions of affection, public and otherwise, were regarded as a natural consequence of both physical and spiritual energies. The laws they instituted were not that complex, as conditions in the kingdom made acts of violence and thievery unthinkable. Education was conducted by the Circle of the Wise with emphasis placed on the learning of Calderont's history and traditions. Whatever technology they enjoyed was designed to improve the quality of life of all citizens and to leave their environment, as much as possible, pristine and unspoiled.

A reverence for nature was at the source of their faith. Whatever was consumed was replaced. Stone rather than wood was used for both domestic and public buildings. Trees were not only preserved but revered. And beauty was almost an obsession. Public and private gardens were rich in floral design, with artificial waterfalls, ponds, and ornamental trees common throughout the realm. And the feast was not just for the eyes. An intoxicating bouquet of flowers and redolent shrubbery daily lifted the senses.

Until now all was good. With the exception of the desolation incurred during the brief raid by the Dragon of Maladour, the people led contented lives. In fact, many viewed the destruction of the Dragon of Maladour by the current king as evidence of the indestructibility of this people. All was restored in short order. The boy who overcame the dragon ascended the throne as a reward from Queen Beldonia's father, King Althius, for accomplishing this feat. The young hero was given the name "Salasand," which in their language meant "orphan," as he was raised without parents.

Salasand's union with Queen Beldonia produced an extraordinary and gifted daughter, Chrysallia, who now faced the crisis of her life. Her birth, celebrated far and wide in Calderont, had occurred at about the time when refugees from surrounding kingdoms began to flee the ceaseless wars, poverty, and persecutions that defined their world. Many never survived the trek through the Desert of Zod and the badlands of Fendor. They were driven not only by a need to escape the self-destructive systems of their kingdoms but also because the tales of their ancient myths spoke of an idyllic land beyond the forested horizons where there was bounty, solace, and harmony.

With little to lose, inhabitants from these warring kingdoms packed what they could and risked life and limb for a better tomorrow. Some made it to Calderont, and while they were eager to conform to the traditions and laws of this promised land, they still harbored hatred and ill will toward those of their world with whom they had conflict. The source of this antipathy was rooted in a belief that their physical characteristics and religious preferences were superior to others. This gave them a sense of entitlement that justified the violence and exploitation they rendered on their foes. Their worlds were also exclusively governed by men.

It was not uncommon for these "vasciste," or miscreants, as they were called by the Calderi, to disrupt the common good with acts of violence toward one another. They also did not respect the natural environment of Calderont and began to fell trees and kill animals sacred to the people. They did not feel a connection to the ground upon which they walked. All this outraged the Calderi. Many wanted to drive them out. Some went so far as to advocate the wholesale slaughter of these intruders. Sadly, the Calderi became the thing they hated.

Good Queen Beldonia had felt otherwise. While she was alive, she arranged for the instruction of all the newcomers in the covenants of the Calderi. She focused on the children and required that they be schooled in the spirit beliefs that constituted the common customs of the land. She modeled the tolerance she requested from them, and it began to work. They loved the queen and slowly came to understand the benefits of a value system that promoted harmony for them all. Disruptions grew less and less.

Then it happened. On an excursion to visit a colony of the newcomers, the queen contracted an ailment uncommon to the Calderi. She went into a quick decline and shortly expired. The populace blamed the "vasciste" as bearers of pestilence, and the "vasciste" in turn prepared to defend themselves against the onslaught they knew was sure to come.

In the face of this, Chrysallia, now in her fifteenth year, was forced to act. Her father, King Salasand, was paralyzed by the death of his wife. When he killed the Dragon of Maladour, he was regarded as one of the greatest heroes in the entire history of Calderont. Yet the circumstances of his life were unique to fighting dragons and little else. He was never prepared to rule. That was the province of the queen, and he gladly acceded to her. Now that she was gone, he was doubly devastated. He lost the thing in life he loved most, and to the great consternation of the people, he could not conduct the affairs of government either. His status and reputation plummeted from the moment the queen grew sick. The land was bordering on chaos, and he became more paralyzed physically and mentally with each passing day. His conflicted mind had but one place that afforded him any esteem or reason for living—his past.

He had lost his parents as a young child and was reared by Drougen, the Guardian of the Woodlands, in a modest hut at the edge of the Forest of Maladour where the dragon would eventually reside. His instruction began at an early age and centered on crossing the forest thresholds of Maladour, which lie at the eastern end of Calderont. Maladour was separated from the Forest of Fendor by a mountain chain called Galamore, which meant "spine" in their language. It was believed that its peaks scraped the very heavens themselves. And the highest of them all was the Tor of Magadorn, unscalable except for birds and bats that used its inaccessibility as secure breeding grounds. It was here that the dragon retreated after it had captured the then Princess Beldonia and the store of gold amassed by good King Althius.

The dragon was bent on revenge. During the creation of the world of Calderont, the gods had imprisoned it for fear that its chaotic nature would disrupt the order necessary for the Calderi to thrive. They consigned it to the forbidding swamp below the Magadorn, assured that it would remain in the mire forever. But the energies of this mystical beast enabled it to escape. To avenge itself against its tormentors, the dragon struck at the source of the Calderi's very existence, their belief that their safety was secured through the worship of these forces of light. If the dragon could fracture these beliefs, the gods would cease to exist, and the dragon would be at the center of a new cosmic system where its primacy as the first form created would be restored.

Famished from eons of confinement, the dragon raided the crops and orchards of the Calderi just before the harvest. It was then that the beast manifested itself physically to them. It had three heads, which could be transformed into any image that the viewer feared, thus paralyzing anyone unfortunate enough to encounter its gaze. Its wings were uniquely ribbed to accommodate spiny appendages with funnels that allowed the air to rush through them. When the dragon dove at great speed, it sounded like ominous pipe organs forecasting doom.

As the days grew short, the cupboards of the Calderi grew bare. No one ventured forth for fuel either for fear that they would see this terrifying beast. They began to freeze and starve. All they could do was pray to the gods for relief. It was then that good King Althius acted.

He turned to the pigeons he had raced when he was a boy. They loved him and were anxious to help in any way they could. The king attached a proclamation to the claw of each and charged them with visiting every home and hovel in the kingdom. The proclamation read: "To any hero brave enough to rid the realm of the Dragon of Maladour, I will give my daughter's hand in marriage and release the gold I have amassed to enrich the good people of Calderont."

But no one came forth. All services public and otherwise ceased. The land was razed. Communication and social intercourse between and among the people ended. The world they knew was coming to an end. It seemed the dragon was avenged.

At the edge of the Forest of Maladour lived the orphan boy, Salasand. He was regarded by young and old alike as a most eccentric child because of his frequent incursions into these forbidden woods. This was done at the urging of Drougen, the holy man, who knew the boy would grow stronger and more powerful every time he breached a threshold into this magical domain. And it was true. Every time Salasand emerged from his excursions he appeared wild eyed to all who saw him. There were rumors that he conversed with animal spirits, inherited their powers, and communed with the forces within Maladour unseen by the eyes of those who lived within the villages and hamlets of Calderont.

Drougen always instructed Salasand to re-enter the forest at a different interval and where it was thickest and most impenetrable. This, Drougen exclaimed, would reveal the most profound truths, because that which was unexplored on the physical plain would release the hidden potentials from the world within. Drougen explained that this journey was the same for all those of a heroic nature and the only course to self-discovery. That which was familiar had to be abandoned in order to lead an authentic life. Salasand in his eagerness absorbed it all.

When one of the pigeons of King Althius flew into his hovel with the proclamation, Salasand took his leave of Drougen and, true to his instruction, sought entrance at a place most forbidding, for he knew this would lead him to the dragon. After several leagues he came upon a stand of densely needled evergreen trees. The world of the unexplored was now unfolding, for in front of him was an archway wide enough to enter, as if some unseen woodsman had carved through the intertwining boughs to give him access to that which lay beyond. Without hesitation he plunged through.

As he cleared the obstructing foliage, he was immediately confronted by a lone wolf of savage demeanor. Instead of attacking, the wolf licked his hand, bounded a few yards, and then returned as if to tell the boy to follow. After a day-long ascent past several icy and frothy rapids framed in the gray mist common to the backwater forest in gloomy Maladour, Salasand and his lupine guide reached the base of the Magadorn. Salasand looked up and shuddered. While the lower façade had enough vegetation to ensure firm footing, once past the tree line the mountain seemed to abandon its connection to all things animate. Its peak was hidden by ominous low-lying clouds midway up its outer crust, and the walls constituting its circumference from this point skyward could not be scaled by any creature without wings. The screeching of raptors flapping toward their nests with struggling prey in their talons foreshadowed the fate of any who dared to leave a footprint in this place of portent. It was clear there was no point of ascent to be found.

Without hesitation the wolf continued leading Salasand around the lower reaches of the Magadorn. Just beyond a stretch of moss-encrusted boulders, Salasand espied a break in the impenetrable stone barricades that hid the inner pathway to the peak where the young man was convinced he would face his dragon. The entrance was wreathed in cobwebs, and foul, reeking odors wafted from its inner sanctum. A whistling sound from the rush of air escaping the mountain's innards intimated that the stones were alive and that the mountain was panting from other openings within its limitless expanse.

Fashioning a torch from the boughs of evergreens that flanked this only opening in Magadorn's granite like composite, Salasand burned off the silken webbing and entered. The wolf followed. Salasand's eyes widened as the contents of the cavern came into view. There were bones strewn upon the floor. Some looked human while others were of beasts of enormous proportions. What struggles must have ensued here, he thought, as man and monster contended for the sanctuary afforded by this womblike enclosure. With fire pits of ringed stone carved into the base of the cavern's floor, it was clear to Salasand that the humans had won.

He was immediately struck with a revelation. This was the ancestral home of the Calderi. He had by no coincidence discovered the source of his people's origins. This is where it all started, he mused. From this stony font his history began, and the pictographs on the walls confirmed this impression. Scenes of cosmic forces conjoining to shape the universe of the Calderi unfolded before him. He traced from panel to panel the events leading to the creation of animal and human form. The acquisition of fire, the demigods who became the patrons of Calderont, the advent of agriculture, and the protocols for entering an afterlife were dramatically portrayed on these canvas-like walls.

As the final frame came into view his hair stood on end, for there was a representation of the dragon of the universe being slain by a young man not unlike himself, and it was clear to him that this last display marked the event that had led the Calderi out of their caves into their current homeland. An era and way of life had ended with the slaying of this earthbound monster. Now he wondered if he were chosen to accomplish a similar end.

As his torch began to flicker out, he noticed a shadowy reflection gently swaying on the stony surface above his head. In shock he instinctively jumped back to see a sword like no other suspended on a tether from an unseen origin high up in the cavern. He quickly jumped to the ledge behind it and put the last flickers of flame to the tether. The sword fell like a lightning bolt, and as he traced its trajectory in the fading light, he saw it split open what looked like a marble case. On the floor next to the embedded sword was a mask that looked like a replica of his own face. With his light almost gone, he affixed the mask, which fit exactly to the contour of his brow, cheeks, and chin. In the moment that his dying torch left both him and the wolf in total darkness, the strangest thing occurred.

As he stared at the wall, powerful beams from the eye slits in the mask illuminated the entire base of the cavern. He then concentrated hard on a rocky slab without any depiction, and to his amazement, the beams burned holes right through it until the entire section gave way and crashed onto the ledge below. The ledge too collapsed. As the dust settled, there before him was a staircase leading to the top of Magadorn.

Salasand was stunned. This could not be coincidence, he thought. Was this journey anticipated and was he, a poor orphan boy, chosen to fulfill this most fearsome task? Would he change the course of history like his predecessor?

Kneeling, he whispered a prayer of gratitude to his guardian spirits and his dead parents whom he believed never really left his presence. With a mighty effort he liberated the sword from its stony encasement. Its surface was luminous, with two funnel-like slits extending at the hilt. As he swung it with force, the sound from the funnels was as frightening as the discordant siren screeches emanating from the dragon's wings. To test its mettle, he came down forcefully on a stony abutment protruding over the stairwell and partially blocking his path. It collapsed almost to dust as he brought the full weight of his swing to bear on the rock. Now he was ready.

With the mask providing light, he and the wolf began the ascent to where he knew the dragon had its lair. As they neared the Tor of Magadorn, the reek of the dragon's breath forced them both to recoil. Before them were three entrances, any of which could house the monster. Unfortunately for the beast, its own odor betrayed it.

Taking the opening to the left, Salasand fell upon the dragon with the fury of a panther. The sword penetrated deep through the hideous scales, and the dragon bellowed so loudly the floor vibrated. Cramped in the tight space of its confinement, it found movement difficult. The dragon knew if it could just bring one of its three heads to confront his attacker, the moment their eyes met the boy would turn to stone in fear.

With a lash of its gigantic tail, the dragon blew out a stand of boulders at the outside entrance to the den and now had room to bring all three of its heads directly to bear on this foolhardy child who had the audacity to confront it. All three heads surrounded the boy so that no matter which direction he chose, the inevitable and fatal gaze would fall on him.

The dragon was stunned to see the boy actually engaging its glance. It experienced panic for the first time, for the beams from the boy's mask began to burn each set of eyes into a gory and scalding gel. The dragon's agony was compounded by the ominous clarion from the slashing sword. What it had done to others was now being done to it, and in short order it expired. Salasand, covered in its blood, hurled the fractured limbs off the Tor back to the swamp from whence the dragon came. The gods of Calderont were avenged.

What Salasand didn't know was that its blood would be the dragon's revenge on him, for he would have no other triumph after this. As he retreated from the lair, he felt a coldness possess him. He looked at the gore on his hands and chest and was repelled. The wolf led him to a cascade formed by the melting ice and frequent rains common to Maladour. The dragon and the raptors that inhabited the Tor used it as a water source. Salasand let the icy rush cleanse him. He felt better.

Retreating back to the middle entrance of the cavern, he espied the glow and glisten of the king's gold. He would later lead an expedition back to Magadorn to retrieve it. Despite his relative poverty, gold held little attraction to him, for it was the currency of power and governance, things that held little interest for him.

His next task was to liberate the princess. He knew from King Althius's proclamation that he now could claim her hand. Yet for all his valor and acumen in the ways of forest and animal energies, Salasand had experienced precious little love in his short life. True, Drougen was a warm and inspiring sage, but beyond this limited relationship, he had not felt the touch of a woman other than his mother, who was a distant memory, having died when he was an infant. He began to shake. His confidence, so prominent when confronting the dragon, left him. There were no weapons to assist him when dealing with matters of the heart.

Steeling himself, he entered the third entrance to his right. There, bound to a stony pillar, was the most compelling sight he had ever seen. Intuitively, he sensed that Princess Beldonia's beauty resonated from an inner virtue that illuminated all of her physical attributes. That aura of kindness restored him. She was shaking from the horrific sounds emanating from the dragon's den during its fatal struggle with Salasand. She thought her time had come. But instead of the dragon's claw at her throat, there stood her liberator.

The young man removed his mask. He immediately seemed to grow taller and more sinewy. There was a light about him too that expelled any anxiety in her as to his own purity or intentions. With his sword he shattered the pillar of stone confining her and the bonds that held her in place. As he gently brought her to her feet, the love between them was immediate, and they kissed as heroes and princesses are wont to do.

Upon their return to Calderont, there were wild celebrations and games that lasted for weeks. The land was restored. And true to his promise, good King Althius conducted the marriage ceremony anointing them both as his heirs.

Salasand's wedding night profoundly affected him. He had a store of sorrow and loss that never found expression. As his wife took him in her embrace and they became one, the wellspring of denial and solitude that had silently scarred him broke. He cried tears of joy and tears of remorse for his lost youth. His wife became his savior far more than his reclamation of her from the dragon's grasp. That was a single event. She saved him every day. And Beldonia felt his anguish, which inspired her to love him even more deeply. She sang to him, wrote poetry for him, and showered him with affection. He relished it all and was happy, truly happy for the first time in his life. Their union produced a daughter who they aptly named Chrysallia.

Salasand had but one legacy to give, and it would be his final accomplishment before the dragon's blood robbed him of will and capacity. He had no investment in things material nor did he find any appeal in commerce. The Calderi, on the other hand, were an enterprising lot. They were keen entrepreneurs, and the trade and transaction between their rural and urban centers was vigorous. This was a life to which he had no exposure.

While the Calderi shunned the more tabooed reaches of the forests as much as possible, Salasand found sanctuary in the quietude of its glens and streams. Things mercantile repelled him, as did the tact and protocols associated with courtly politics. Almost immediately into his reign, he surrendered to his charismatic wife the daily machinations of governmental and commercial affairs. The queen was perfectly suited for this responsibility. Unlike her husband, her life was steeped in the traditions and rituals of her people. She was always present with her father for religious ceremonies, dedications of public buildings, charitable efforts to lift the poor to higher station, oversight of the educational institutes, and as the official greeter of delegations who regularly came to court seeking favors or bearing gifts for the beneficence they received from the king.

Beldonia was revered for her love of Calderont and its citizenry, which defined her every act. When King Althius passed, the amity and prosperity of the realm was further enhanced. The queen was always accessible, just in all her dealings, yet firm in demanding from her councils and ministers the highest standards of service to the people.

Salasand was loved for other reasons. The sword and mask were displayed above his throne as reminders that any force threatening the prosperity and peace of the kingdom would be dealt with by the boy who became king. He was the army they never needed, and all was well in this dynamic between the king and queen. They had settled into a relationship that worked for them and the denizens of Calderont.

As time passed, Salasand grew restless and uncomfortable. He had an increasing sense of foreboding and felt an urgency to leave some legacy other than wealth to the people he also loved. His heart was always with the children, because more than any other in the realm, he felt the sting and anguish of abandonment at a tender age. The thought of any youth being unprepared for the inevitable misfortunes to which all were sure to be called troubled him greatly. His only solace when in these circumstances was the wisdom tendered to him by the sage, Drougen. He vowed to return the favor.

He would give to the young people of Calderont that which he had received. On the feast day of the passing of the Dragon of Maladour, King Salasand would assemble groups of children and guide them to some secret place in Fendor or Maladour. The inevitable spark of transformation was experienced with every crossing of a forest boundary for the first time. A sense of expanding their former confinement as villagers infected them more than anything they could have experienced from their learning institutions. This was especially underscored whenever they came upon a cave because Salasand would whisper to them that in a time of doubt that which was needed would be embedded there, and he would brandish the sword and mask as proof of his point.

None relished these excursions more than his daughter, Princess Chrysallia. All that her father obtained from his initiations into these forbidden worlds she readily absorbed. She was no stranger to the creatures of these woodland precincts cither. While shunning most humans, the animals would instinctively nuzzle her as if she were one of their own.

But she was not just her father's daughter. Queen Beldonia adored her as well and began to tutor her not unlike the way Drougen had tutored her husband. Beldonia's mystique was centered in her capacity to penetrate the innermost thoughts and feelings of her people. And since her motivation was to love and support, all who came before her showed a vulnerability usually reserved for their most intimate relationships. Beldonia enjoyed unusual loyalty as a result. The good queen was intent on passing this legacy on to her daughter because, having only one heir, it was imperative that the princess be ready should crisis or misfortunes disturb the common good of Calderont. In this she was secure, for Chrysallia had superseded her mother's gift, because she enjoyed equal access to mysteries beyond things human from her father.

CHAPTER 2:
A KING ABDICATES

The final delegation of the grief stricken took their farewell from the form that was once Queen Beldonia. They gave obeisance to King Salasand and the young princess, and as all the others extended their condolences, one among them, Pentamon, a member of the Circle of the Wise, came forward and asked the king for an audience after the entombment of the queen. With great foreboding the king agreed. He would have a week to prepare as the funereal rituals would take that long.

That evening he asked his servants to leave him to his chambers. He assumed the sitting position he always took when he wanted to find that layer of consciousness beyond the worldly plane. There he always found his answers.

He knew he had to craft a course of action to prevent the imminent collapse of his kingdom. The incursion of these foreigners and the conflicting belief systems they embraced sowed discord between and among the factions that represented them and had begun to impact directly on the Calderi themselves. Some Calderi wanted the foreigners expelled to preserve their way of life. Some wanted them exterminated altogether. The queen and many others had viewed these wretches with compassion because they were seeking refuge from the very behavior they now exhibited. If they could be shown a better way, good Queen Beldonia had been convinced their celebration of the Calderi way of life would be more greatly valued than their own native peoples who inherited such beneficence.

King Salasand was torn. His impulse was to attack as he had attacked the Dragon of Maladour. "But these are people, not dragons," he mused, "and my beloved wife took their part. I must find a balance, a strategy that will lead to a desired outcome. But how?"

The king's life had not prepared him for crises of this sort. He could not command, and he knew not how to negotiate. Plus, he felt the coldness of the dragon's blood robbing him daily of strength no matter how much he fought it. His legs could barely support him.

"He may take my body," he reflected, "but he shall not claim my spirit. I will sit and wait for my answer to come."

No matter the level of concentration or the review of stratagems, this would be the first time his effort to find an answer failed. His mind retreated to the only thing that really mattered to him—the loss of his beautiful wife. She was irreplaceable. Regardless of how he breathed or slowed his heart rate, the thought of her haunted him. He would see her visage in every mundane act they shared, in the blush of the lavender and white flowers she planted in the window boxes that lined the casements below their marriage bed, to the very stars themselves glistening as if they were created to mirror the expanse of affection that these two had held for each other.

His anguish grew even greater when he rolled to the side of their bed to feel the reassuring presence of her body only to find a strand of her hair and a cold sheet where once she had lain. It was as if a physical part of him had been taken. The weight of his grief, the scope of the impending crisis, and the creeping malaise from the dragon's blood sapped him of strength. He wept and dreamt of death, his new lover, who would bring him peace or oblivion. His inner voice cried out: "My beloved, why did you leave me when I loved you most? Help me. Send me a sign."

In that moment Princess Chrysallia quietly entered his room. She saw his broken body framed in the full light of the summer moon, which stood in contrast to her own regal bearing. He sensed her presence, and with eyes still glistening, he engaged her glance. That she should see him like this when but a few years earlier he was tossing her playfully in the full complement of manly vigor only compounded his anguish.

Hiding her own grief at her mother's passing, Chrysallia went to her father. Embracing him, she gave a comfort only those who mutually suffer an equal loss can share. She wept tears unseen by the only man she adored. She murmured in his ear: "I will help you."

The king, though desperate, least expected that help could come from one so untested. "My daughter, you have seen but fifteen years. The kingdom will soon be in chaos if this crisis with these foreigners isn't resolved. I have to act."

"What do you wish to accomplish, Father?" she asked.

He turned to meet her question, and then, averting his gaze from her eyes, he exclaimed, "I am not sure." Chrysallia's insight into the human spirit far exceeded his own even when she was a child. She inherited from each parent their own unique mystiques, and in this sense she was more evolved than them both. But this capacity was yet to be observed until this moment.

"I know what to do," she uttered confidently. Her father's eyes widened. "I must meet with the leadership of these interlopers and discover the sources of their animosity. Then I must leave Calderont and illuminate these alien kingdoms in the values of our way of life or the grief they foster will result in a never ending flood of them escaping their world and destroying ours."

King Salasand was now doubly alarmed. He had just lost his wife. Now he stood to lose a daughter as well. "You cannot do this, my daughter. If you leave, I am utterly alone. I need you here to help me. The allegiances of our ministers and the Circle of the Wise are more aligned to your mother and you. I always prayed I would die before her. Now the whirlwind is upon us. You cannot leave. I forbid it."

She waited a long moment, understanding his fear. "Father, I will meet with Pentamon and the Circle of the Wise in a week. I will charge them with the preservation of the kingdom, and I will instruct them on exactly how I want that done. I have long reflected on the way we govern, and I have found a way to lift this awful burden from you. Responsibility for the well-being of our realm must be shared, and to that end I will give direction, but not before I meet with the priests and ministers of the 'vasciste.'"

He looked at his daughter as if for the first time. She was just over fifteen years of age, stood five-and-a-half feet tall, her body taut from her climbs up the lower ranges of the Galamore chain, with eyes that could strip the resistance to her will in a flash. He intended to resist those eyes, for his new dragon had him in its grips, and he verged on panic. "You cannot go. If I lose you, my reason for staying alive is gone."

She returned his frantic glare with arms firmly crossed, her chin slightly elevated, and her silky black hair carelessly tossed over her right shoulder. "If I don't go, no one in Calderont will have a reason for staying alive. These intruders are desperate. From what I have already learned, their world is close to collapse. Their resources are consumed; their habitats polluted from their greed; their children are neglected and violent, and war is the principal solution to all their problems. Soon there will be an avalanche of them who will despoil our world as well. Tell me you wish this for us, Father, and I will stay."

She broke his will. He could not say no and be a king responsible for a people. Sadly he nodded and asked her to take leave of him. He wanted to be alone.

As she reached the door to exit his chamber, she turned only to face the back of him, for he could not look at her. "Father, I need your authority to release the home guard to me so that I may force the 'vasciste' to accede to my will. Without their compliance, my plan to preserve Calderont in my absence will fail."

Refusing to turn, he responded in a husky voice, "You have it."

"Thank you, Father…I want to tell you something. Will you look at me?" He turned unwillingly to face her. "Father, I could not go forth to face this dragon if you had not taught me how you faced yours. My love for you remains in Calderont. And your love goes with me into the forest, as does Mother's. Please do not let me go without your blessing."

"My precious child, come to me." She ran now as the little girl who did not have to be strong to receive the hug of a father who was king. They embraced a long time.

While she trembled in the final embrace of her childhood, strength and resolve began to flow back into him. In the arms of his only daughter he found the stream he was looking for. Destiny must be served, and it was a lesson learned from a child. In letting go he found a measure of peace. Joyfully she kissed him and as always made him laugh as she ran out the door.

CHAPTER 3:
THE SOURCE OF THE STORM

Of all the public buildings in Calderont, Chrysallia loved the Hall of the Covenant the best. Its tall columns supported a pediment depicting scenes from her father's battle with the Dragon of Maladour and were wreathed in garlands of flowering vines, which were tended to every day by the keepers of the temple. At the base of each pillar were four decorative urns partially hidden by cascades of multicolored blooms and tendrils draping over their sides almost to the flooring. They stood in stark contrast to the somber message within. It was here that she decided to meet the leadership of each of the "vasciste" so that she might learn the source of their dark history with each other before her quest to their native lands.

She directed the home guard to bring a delegation from each of the tribes to her father's throne at the rear altar of the great hall just after dawn the next morning. She knew this was a time when, fresh from sleep, they would be most disposed to relate to what she was seeking. She also knew they would be expecting the king instead of the princess, so she decided to dress as regally as possible. Borrowing from her mother's wardrobe, she selected a lavender and white robe with a brocade of forest flowers across her right breast. With her hair pulled up and a single braid draped over her right shoulder to meet the gold beads of the blossoms, she looked like a goddess.

The tension in Calderont was festering because of the passing of Queen Beldonia. Normally a peaceful people, the Calderi felt so threatened by these alien entities within their border that hordes of their youth, both male and female, were joining the home guard. Soon the guard, which was instituted as a light police force, swelled to an army. Chrysallia did not have much time.

Her first task before meeting the tribal ambassadors was to convene and seek guidance from the Circle of the Wise. As the most educated and insightful of the people, they dedicated themselves to learning in all its forms, with a distinct eye to garnering from each discipline that which would best serve the culture of the Calderi. They had obtained the sacred scripts of each alien tribe and were able to translate them into their own language. This was accomplished ironically through the children of these foreigners. While attending Calderi schooling, these youth quickly picked up the language of their adopted land. Almost all of them carried the sacred books at the insistence of their parents and priests lest they become contaminated by the heresies of their peers. The children in their innocence were more than happy to share their knowledge of these anointed texts with their Calderi teachers. This would prove invaluable to Chrysallia in her quest.

She dedicated the day and evening prior to her meeting to learn these mysteries. No one had a greater grasp of these conflicting mythologies then Pentamon, the pontiff of the Circle of the Wise. She knew she would have to reveal her plans to him for the governance of the kingdom within the week and before her leave-taking. The future of Calderont lay in the balance of what a fifteen-year-old princess could learn from the wisest in the realm in so brief an expanse of time. All would be affected by her decision upon her departure.

Pentamon met her in her chambers carrying six tomes constituting the metaphysical core of a world yet unknown to the Calderi. He was agitated. "Highness, what I have learned from these texts is sobering indeed. There is inspiration, possibility, and goodness in them all except for one thing."

"And what would that be?" Chrysallia exclaimed tentatively.

"Intolerance," Pentamon revealed sadly. "All these works address the creation of their world, a male deity as its author, messengers anointed to reclaim the lost and reveal the truth, the protocols for redemption, daily prescriptions for diet and things unclean, and the regimens necessary to be in favor with a cosmic Father."

Chrysallia was befuddled. "I really don't see much that is harmful in any of that. Why then do they hate and fear each other so?"

Pentamon succinctly relayed the source of all that festered in their world. "From what I can see, the one thing that is not embraced by any of these works is that their Creator made them different and is equally committed to them all. Unfortunately, each claims an exclusive relationship with this force. They imagine that there is only one Truth and that they have been anointed to promulgate it.

"Any variation is a heresy. Any refusal to accept that divinely authored enlightenment will lead to the damnation of the nonbeliever. They have committed barbarous acts on each other, forced conversions and wholesale slaughter of peoples because of deviations from what each considers the true revelation. They call their deity by many names, yet he is the same in all these works.

"They have common sacred places that they refuse to share. They are willing to kill and willing to die for ground that is fertilized daily by their blood. The earth, which in their earlier mythologies was female, is completely exploited and despoiled. Their air is befouled, their waters tainted, and their forests are being depleted to their ultimate destruction. Greed and power backed by violence or its threat preoccupy their rulers.

"Sadly, their sky god does not reside in the earth they trod, so these things are done with impunity. For some, women are the source of their fallen condition. Their attractiveness and sexuality, which we celebrate, are perceived as especially distracting and dangerous and must be curtailed. There are revolutions against this all over parts of their world."

Chrysallia was repelled and felt an anger growing in her not unlike the rest of the Calderi who saw in these tenets the ultimate defacing of their own lands. Yet even for her tender age she knew that if she reacted in kind, she would join them in the same dark dance.

Pentamon then offered some possibility of hope. "In all these requisitions, however, there are two beliefs that could move them to a spiritual plane where all their conflicts would be resolved. There is at the source of all these texts an imperative to love the force and energy of the universe, which they call God, and an equal imperative to love each other. If somehow they could see, or someone could make them see, that all are equally invested by this source, millennia of grief would come to an end."

Chrysallia was about to ask Pentamon how a positive and common belief could become so clouded and who could possibly benefit from such a departure to a universal good. And then she heard a commotion below her window. There in the courtyard one of the priests of the "vasciste" was dragging a little boy away from one of his peers who was dressed differently and of a different shade of skin. He was admonishing the child, who was crying from the interruption of frolic with what was to him just another little playmate. The priest began to warn the child of how he would be endangering his soul, in fact his whole association with his parents and people, if he continued to engage in such behavior. As he was being pulled in one direction by the priest, the boy turned around to see his companion sadly waving good-bye.

And then it came to her. It was the priests. They had the most to gain by controlling the belief systems of the people. If they were the sole intermediaries between worshipers and their God, they would wield immense power and influence. Rituals could enforce this, and keeping the tribes separated would prevent contamination of thought by other disciplines. It would also establish the necessary barriers that would inhibit any questioning that could come from gaining other perspectives. Obedience was the virtue most celebrated by these well-meaning caretakers. Anyone who disobeyed was deemed a threat to their culture. Isolation also ensured that the populace from these diverse communities would never be aware of their overriding commonality. A parochial view of the world replaced a spiritual one, thus ensuring a perpetuation of their authority.

The Calderi by contrast communed with their ultimate energy directly. Their priests aided in this, but without the imposition of dogma. As a result they saw divinity in earth and sky, male and female, human and beast, tree and stone. Balance and harmony permeated their perceptions of the Spirit Force and of themselves.

Armed with this critical insight, Chrysallia steeled herself for the morning meeting with the "vascite." She arrived early dressed in her mother's royal robe and took her seat on her father's throne. The home guard who had earlier informed the delegates to assemble at the appointed hour escorted them with weapons brandished to the great hall of Salasand.

As the troupe passed the vestibule of the edifice, they were awestruck by the somber interior, which belied the promise of the entrance outside. The roof supported a dome with a small opening at its apex to allow some sunlight, but not enough to distract the worshiper from his or her proper reflection, which confronted him or her at the walls and altar of this imposing structure. Scenes from the Calderi's history and the divine participants symbolically portrayed in its formation were beautifully painted on the walls so the worshipers became immediately conscious of the world that existed beyond forms. The Calderi knew their metaphors were masks of that which could not be seen or felt. The goal was to have a mystical experience where the inner voices inherent in all could become activated. There was just enough light to create the eerie effect necessary for such transport.

As they made their way down the aisle to the throne, they were shocked by two things. One was the presence of a girl, albeit a beautiful one and a princess, waiting to greet them. To most it was an insult not to be met by the king himself. In their cultures, children, especially female children, should be preoccupied with other things than affairs of state.

The other presence that caught their eye was the huge Sword and Mask of Salasand at each side of the throne. It gave most of them pause as they knew full well the power of these weapons. Above the throne was the scene that showed the death throes of the Dragon of Maladour as the young Salasand penetrated its scaly armor to extinguish its life. As their eyes naturally followed this panorama to its grisly end, they saw written there in the boldest of print the following declaration: "THE MOST DESTRUCTIVE DRAGONS ARE THE ONES THAT LIE WITHIN."

But one among them was not intimidated. He saw opportunity. The Sword of Salasand was too large for even a man to wield, much less a girl, the mask a useless artifact. He would wait for an opening.

Chrysallia convened the meeting and asked that each ambassador identify himself, his people, and the reason for their incursion into Calderont. She was fascinated by the look of them. All had a different hue to the skin and were of varying heights and physiques. While they were somewhat resentful to be commanded by a child, they complied. After all, they were in another people's territory. Why provoke unnecessarily, they thought. If they could grow in numbers and influence, they might gain advantage.

The Calderi were not warlike. Their land was rich in all manner of resources with plentiful supplies of food, arable land, and great stores of peat for fuel. In time, each thought, they could gain ascendancy over these untutored, untested dreamers. The problem was how they could gain dominance over each other.

What they did not anticipate was Chrysallia's capacity to see through them. She fed their fears by baiting them to relate their grievances toward one another. In that instant scheming and rationality left them. There were no more thoughts of rebellion, for as long as they were at each other's throats, the Calderi were safe, or so she thought.

In the midst of this chaos, Viladon, leader of the Terruleans, a savage people with a history for violence and persecution, saw his chance. His tribe was by far the most populous in Calderont. They were also the most contentious. Viladon had been battle tested and without mercy in the face of his enemies. He had killed children, massacred the innocent, and taken land-all in the name of the totem deity who he believed endorsed his and his people's butchery for higher cause.

Knowing King Salasand's incapacity due to the queen's passing, he correctly assessed that a token home guard could not prevent a preemptive take over by his chieftains. He was not aware that the Calderi were preparing for just such an eventuality, nor was he aware of Chrysallia's incredible powers.

Without hesitation, he rushed the throne to take Chrysallia hostage. He would bend this innocent, naive girl to his will, escape to the forest, and force her to become his bride, willingly or not, and then return to ensure his succession to the throne of Calderont. When she experienced the power of his manhood, she would comply as women from the Terruleans were conditioned to do. The other tribes would yield to him—or else, and the Calderi would be overrun with little resistance. Or so Viladon the Terrulean thought.

Before he reached the marble base upon which rested the throne of Salasand, Chrysallia had already unsheathed the sword that killed the Dragon of Maladour. The rage in her was unleashed. She caught him where his collar bone met his shoulder and severed his arm. Viladon, still conscious, shrieked like the many innocents he himself had butchered.

The delegation recoiled in horror and unanticipated shock. For a moment all seemed frozen. The arm of Viladon had reached the beveled edge of the marble stand supporting the throne, and all eyes followed the horrific drop of this gory appendage. And then they looked up to see Chrysallia waving in a violent circular motion the Sword of Salasand as she severed the arrogant head from Viladon's disfigured body. It toppled down to where the ambassadors were seated, eyes open and mouth contorted from the last conscious shriek of the once proud Terrulean.

Chrysallia calmly picked it up by the hair and gave it to Viladon's second. "Take this back to your people and tell them my name is Chrysallia, daughter of Salasand the Dragon Slayer and Beldonia the Merciful. They can have one or the other, for if you do not yield to my sovereignty, your blood will give new life to our gardens and arbors. You who have not shown mercy will receive none."

Then she turned on the rest of them. She brandished the siren-sounding Sword of Salasand so the discordant blasts from the funnels at the hilt could be heard all the way to the Tor of Magadorn itself. The entire hall shook from a cacophony of thunder and wail that left every delegate frozen, deaf, and horrified to the point of death.

Turning her back on the prostrate wretches, she placed her father's weapon upon her knees as she sat once again on the throne. Viladon's minion was already racing to the camp where the Terruleans were billeted with Viladon's head still dripping blood from the severed arteries that had fueled the sinister machinations of this once fabled warrior.

The crippled forms of the remaining delegates slowly revived, though their hearts were racing dangerously from a terror they could not process. They turned to face a girl who could no longer be regarded as a child.

23

"You have a choice," she calmly uttered. "Adopt our ways, give us your children to be educated to possibilities unavailable from your own perverted theologies, or find here in quicker fashion the perpetual misery you have visited upon each other for millennia. It is up to you. Tomorrow you will assemble at the portal to the Forest of Fendor for my instruction. I will depart at sunrise. I must find and enter each of your realms, confront your kings to find common cause, or there will be no end to the flood of you to Calderont. The people will not tolerate that, and we will either have to annihilate you or stop you at your borders. For the sake of all, pray I succeed. I know not what I must face, but I must go. Leave me, share what you have seen and heard, and be at the gate at the sun's own awakening."

The delegates left the altar of the hall numb and shaken. They had gone through so much to get to Calderont, and now they were exposed by what they thought was a child. "Who knows what she is?" they reflected.

And then something mysterious happened. They began to bond with each other because they all faced the same dilemma. The threat of Chrysallia unified them in common cause. All at once they began to converse animatedly: "We can't go back. It is good here. We have no advantage. She will kill us all if we plot against these people. Our past must not be our future. It is time for change. I have not traveled over desert, mountain, and forest to find here what I sought to escape there." They stared at each other in wonder.

While the barbarians experienced a sense of promise, the opposite happened to Chrysallia. As she turned to make sure the sword of her father was clean of the gore of Viladon, she glanced up again at the writing on the wall to read the inscription as if for the first time: THE MOST DESTRUCTIVE DRAGONS ARE THE ONES THAT LIE WITHIN. It was as if the words had been written exclusively for her. Her dragon had won, not her. She had become the thing she hated and resolved her problem in the same fashion as Viladon might have done had he had such an advantage. In some way killing him, however necessary, was tantamount to killing herself. The same terrible enigma that caught her father now had her in its grip. She would need to find redemption in some fashion or she would join the dissipating Salasand on a similar bed.

CHAPTER 4:
A FATHER'S FAREWELL

The fading light of the western sun projected the shimmering shadows of the ornamental trees that lined King Salasand's gardens below the window of his bedchamber. This was his favorite time of day. He loved sunsets and the play of light that seemed to animate the forest creatures embroidered in the tapestry behind his place of rest. It always drew him into a reverie of his days as an untutored youth exploring Calderont's forests and the unspoken secrets of their beauty and energy. The creatures in the canopy of the coniferous treetops down to the courting frogs in the brooks below always kept up a constant banter with him to join in the celebration of life in its purest expression. He held on to this moment, for it was a respite from the grim truth he had to live with every day.

Into this sanctum the somber image of his daughter appeared. Salasand was startled but pleased. "Father, I must speak to you."

Salasand heard the anguish in the voice of his beloved child and beckoned her to him. "Come and sit by me like you used to when I told you nighttime stories all the days of your youth."

Chrysallia could never resist the reassuring embrace of the only man she loved. She nestled into the crease in his shoulder and still fit there perfectly, as if her father's anatomy was designed to accommodate her. "I am deeply frightened, Father. Something happened today in the Great Hall that I did not anticipate. One of the aliens, a man named Viladon from the tribe of Terruleans, tried to take me. I knew, as I have known most of my life, what he intended before his own thoughts prompted him to act. As he rushed the throne, I unhinged your sword and cut off his shoulder and arm.

"I realize now that was all I had to do, and I would have been safe. The man might have even lived and my point would have been made without killing him. And then, Father, as I looked at the faces of these invaders, these disrupters of our comfort, a rage came over me. I cut off his head, picked it up, and handed it to his second in command, a wild, brutal-looking man not unlike himself. I told him to take it back to the Terruleans as a taste of what I would do to them all should they plot against us. I told him who I was and threatened to annihilate them. Then I turned on the delegation and wielded your sword until the wail of it almost killed them all. They were terrified, and I enjoyed it. Then they left."

Salasand jumped to his feet and, even though unsteady, raised his daughter to face him. "Did any of the blood from this man's wounds touch your body?"

"No, Father," she exclaimed.

"You must be sure," he shouted.

"I am sure, Father. Not a drop touched my skin. Why?"

Salasand was trembling as he relived his own agony with the Dragon of Maladour. He struggled whether to tell her of his dark secret or not, especially on the advent of the day she might leave him forever. Yet he had to, for this might be his final chance to prepare her for what was coming. She had to know so she could face the trial that awaited her beyond the boundaries of all that was familiar.

"Chrysallia, the one thing I never wanted you to inherit from me was anger. I tried to give you a life of laughter and learning, a life where the ugly and the cruel could not touch you."

She interrupted him. "But Father, you did."

He silenced her. "I must finish, for the curse that afflicts me must never be visited upon you, and it will if you do not hear me now."

She could hear the urgency in his voice and felt the same compulsion to learn if her fate was to be the same as his. Her silent nod invited him to continue.

"When I entered Maladour to face the dragon, I was met by a wolf. He became my guide to bring me to the thing I had to confront. Once I entered the Cave of the People, I got my hands on the sword and the mask, and I felt power like never before. I knew I could defeat anything and wasn't afraid. I should have been, because it was not the dragon who was my enemy.

"When I reached his lair, I attacked. But it wasn't to save Calderont. It wasn't to release your mother, and it wasn't for the gold or the throne that awaited me. I wanted to kill him because my parents had died and left me without love, without a childhood."

Chrysallia was overcome with compassion and embraced her father. He let her, and in that fashion continued with his tale. "I wanted to kill him because I was the poorest boy in the realm. I wanted to kill him because someone had to pay for that, and there he was. So I wielded the Sword of Invincibility for myself and not the people. I bore out the dragon's eyes with the Mask of Terrors to give him a taste of my own misery. But in the end, it was I who was defeated, because once the dragon's blood was on me, I felt an iciness flare within as I feel it now. It was in that moment that I knew I was not a hero. Heroes conquer themselves first."

Chrysallia was transfixed. "So it was you who wrote the inscription above your throne warning of the dragon within."

He sadly nodded. "Yes. But I learned the lesson too late. I should have gone back to the forest to undergo the trials that could have purged me and left me whole."

"Why didn't you, Father?"

Salasand sighed. "Your mother wouldn't let me, and I was happy in a woman's embrace for the first time in my life. I loved your mother more than any man loved any woman. She was my life. But I should have gone back into the forest for the answers that would have made me complete from within instead of being content with what I had from without. I am paying for that now."

Chrysallia was heartbroken for her father and frightened for herself. "Am I to join you in this journey?"

Salasand shook his head. "No, the blood of the man you killed didn't touch you. And you know what you must not do from my own transgression. At least I could give you that."

Knowing her hour was at hand, Chrysallia sought more from the man she still regarded as the hero of the Calderi. They all would have perished whether he had acted on his own behalf or theirs. "Father, I wish you could be my guide when I enter Fendor."

He took her face in his hands and murmured as if his words were an embrace itself: "But I am. I just can't go with you as your grandfather, good King Althius, knew he could not go with me. Discovery comes when all that you know is left behind and all that you do not know lies in front of you. I believe your destiny is not my destiny. I have learned much in life from my pain. That which governs all life has a plan for all life. This will always be a mystery to us. But there are signs, and if it is our fate to see those signs, life even in its misfortune takes on meaning and, above all, benefit. I see that now."

Chrysallia was befuddled at his last comment. She pressed him: "But Father, how could that be, how could something good come from evil?"

He turned from her as if struggling to be precise in what he was to say. Turning again to face her, he exclaimed, "My dearest, I have looked back on many journeys including my own. In our youth everything is sampled for the first time and life seems like a series of accidents. But as you age, the looking back reveals a pattern not just for you but for others as well. That which you thought was misfortune actually was the wellspring for wisdom, compassion, and growth, especially growth. Messengers for good or for tragedy appear uninvited, and each leaves its own illumination for the one who can see."

Enthralled, Chrysallia felt as if she were seeing her father for the first time. He was wise not from the sacred books but from his own initiations. Drougen the Sage had done well in fostering this. "Father, explain to me how a messenger who is bad can lead us to wisdom."

Salasand smiled with an affirming nod. "When we are hurt, or when we hurt others, something very profound can occur. We get to meet strangers we may not have liked or trusted before. There are among us those whose life experiences far outstrip our own. They have seen more and suffered more. When we fall or are pulled out of that which makes us comfortable, we begin to understand them. We see and feel what they have gone through. They in turn feel kinship with us. Misfortune and what others call evil or sin are the instruments that enable us to measure the good.

"If all that disappeared, you would be unable to appreciate anything. It is in its opposite that good truly becomes experienced. Those that love the most probably have suffered the most. They know what it means to be human. They know that sooner or later we all fail or hurt, and in that they understand us. More than that, they love us. So my precious daughter, know that there is illumination to be inherited from the bad as well as the good. Then there is no waste to life or experience. Triumph or tragedy, you can still win."

At this, a deep calm overcame Chrysallia and fear left her. He interrupted her reflection. "Have I confused you, my child?"

Chrysallia went to him and with a mighty hug made the good king laugh at the strength of her. "I am the most fortunate of children to have you as my father. You are my messenger for life."

The time for departure had arrived. They both knew it and resisted. Salasand said one more thing: "My daughter, when you enter the forest past the final threshold, the magic will begin. Be open to it, and you will get your answers."

She took her leave of him and went to her own bedchamber. On the morrow she would give her instruction to Pentamon and the leaders of the six tribes.

She did not sleep well as she ruminated over what she would say to the assemblage at the Portal to Fendor at dawn's first light. But in that moment when the calming words of her father visited her, fear found its exit. She had a plan, and it was good. If they followed it, there would be no vacuum from her departure in the land of Calderont. If they didn't, she knew from her father's advice that destiny had other things in store for her and for the people, and there was nothing she could do about that. As she rolled over to find her favorite position to sleep, she felt a lump in the covers. It was the stuffed cat creature she had always slept with as a child. It always made her feel safe. She hugged it and fell into a deep sleep.

CHAPTER 5:
A COUNCIL IS CONVENED

As the faint light of dawn reached the Portal of Fendor, Pentamon and the delegation of the tribes assembled as they were commanded. The air was light and not just from the refreshing breezes that always greeted the sunrise in the kingdom of Calderont. The tribal chieftains were exchanging pleasantries and even Pentamon was taken aback by this change of behavior. Their transformation, as he would discover, took place in the sanctum of the Hall of the Covenant. More would follow, for this venue was the centerpiece of Chrysallia's plan for governance in her absence. But all was not well, as the princess would soon find out.

Their early morning ease was broken as the entourage led by Chrysallia and the king's courtiers bearing him in his carriage approached with the clanging of cymbals, the flurry of trumpets, and the loud pulsing of drums. The king was a tragic figure indeed. He could barely walk from his malady and had to be borne to his great embarrassment by the minions of the court for every public occasion.

Not knowing of Chrysallia's plans, the Calderi had a deep sense of foreboding as a result of the void she was creating by the undertaking of this quest. They knew she had to go to confront the greatest threat to their existence since the Dragon of Maladour, but at the same time they were more than aware that the king was unfit to govern. There was no political alternative in Calderi culture to replace him. A great gathering of the people followed the royal train to learn their fate.

Chrysallia began the proceedings by inviting the chieftains to come forward, identify themselves, and pledge their loyalty to her and the Calderi way of life.

A sturdily built man darker in complexion than the rest and dressed in the colorful garb of his people spoke first. "I am Kwalessi of the Compalla people. I am here to acknowledge my clan's gratitude for giving us safe haven, and we are ready to learn your ways so our children can have a life better than what we have given them in the land of our fathers. My people have suffered for centuries under the old ways, as have my comrades here also. We know we must change. You must teach us how. I will give you my loyal pledge to make this happen, and I want to say to my brothers that we will never go forward unless we forgive each other for what we have done in the past. We who suffered greatly at your hands offer you forgiveness, and we seek the same in return."

His statement struck a deep chord with the other tribes. Many were deeply moved and roared their approval at this bold statement. Kwalessi had raised the olive branch first. Many would follow. They knew they had to leave the past and all associated with it, or they would not survive. The group rose to applaud Kwalessi, and he was pleased.

The next to rise was an older man, bearded, with sharp features and of somewhat lighter complexion. His clothes hung loose on him and draped off his shoulders almost to the ground. His eyes hung heavy with sadness as one who has witnessed more than enough tragedy in a lifetime. "My name is Zaid. I am the leader of the tribes of the Riff along the border of Zod. From my youth I have known nothing but conflict. I have lost my brother, a wife, and two male children to wars and persecution. I am tired to the bone. I came to Calderont with my daughter and remaining son. I seek peace, and I will do what is necessary if the rest agree. I pledge to you my loyalty."

He glanced with some reservation at the man who next rose. He looked as if he could be a relative of Zaid, stout of build, keen eyed, and equally weary. "I am Dolgin, an elder from the tribe of Yesh, east of Zod. I too have experienced great loss. My parents and my oldest son have been taken in conflict with our neighbors from the Riff. I want no more of it. If there is a way to peace, I will embrace it. You have my pledge."

The Calderi were shocked, for they could not believe what they were hearing. What magic had Chrysallia wrought in the Hall of the Covenant to fuel such change? What potion did she give them to bring about such transformation? Their spirits lifted. There was hope after all. Or so it seemed.

When Dolgin the Elder took his place, Ramullo the Ligurian stood before the congregation. "I am Ramullo, lord of the Ligurians in Calderont. My story is no different. My people who live far north of your forests were occupied by our enemies for centuries, and we grew to trust no one. Justice did not exist for us. In the current times, there is a conflict of one against the other everywhere. Our lands are dying, and those that lead do nothing. The air is good here. I want to stay. I want my children to have no memory of past grief or fear. I give my pledge to you."

Then he did something startling. He called Kwalessi forward. As the darker man approached him, he extended his hand. Kwalessi's eyes filled with tears. Without a word, for neither could speak, their hands clasped in friendship and forgiveness. A roar went up, for both Calderi and the tribal peers saw what their future could be.

Finally a man of smaller stature and a different shape to the eye came forward and faced Chrysallia. "I am Jiang, leader of the Shui tribe in Calderont. We too were occupied and persecuted for centuries. Then we grew strong and struck fear into our enemies. Our culture is ancient, but we adopted the ways of our exploiters and became like them. Many of us could take it no longer, and we fled. Your land and all its promise is written in books of legend, but no one knew where to find it. We wandered like everyone else through endless desert and forests. Most did not survive. Sadly, we still carried the baggage of our resentments and divisions with us. The old ways were strong, and we sought advantage over you and each other. It wasn't until we felt your wrath for our scheming that enlightenment came to us. When we left the great hall, we knew our future could not be a repeat of our past. We would have to change. I give you my solemn pledge that the people of the Shui will support that change."

Again there was more cheering, but none more than from the tribesmen themselves. The Calderi were used to peace and amity, the clan people were not. The implications for them were truly revolutionary. This was going to work.

Chrysallia scanned the assemblage as she contemplated her next step. Then her optimism left and her blood turned to ice. The Terruleans were not present. She immediately ordered a contingent of light horsemen to go to their camp and compel their attendance. Now she would need all the personal skill inherited from her mother and the insight inherited from her father to stave off any setback. Turning to her subjects, she assured them that the foundation they crafted would go forward regardless of the Terruleans.

There was much discussion among the tribes and the Calderi themselves as to what their absence would mean. In short order the horsemen returned. The Terruleans had broken camp and were nowhere to be found. It was later learned that they had returned to the Hall of the Covenant during the night and recovered the remains of Viladon. There was much consternation within the clans. Some said the Terruleans, the most bellicose of the old order, would seek revenge for the death of Viladon. Others were equally sure that they left in fear when the wrath of Chrysallia was visited upon them. Even the Terruleans would understand the consequences should they entertain conflict.

The more sagacious among them concluded that the Terruleans simply sought refuge elsewhere and would never return. Even the Calderi knew there were other realms beyond the mystical expanse of the great forests. The Terruleans, they assumed, would seek sanctuary in a place where they could more easily impose their will.

Chrysallia did not have the luxury of speculation. Her time was near. She raised her arm and brought the congregation to order. "My loyal subjects," she intoned in a solemn voice, "let us not worry what the Terruleans do. Let us focus on what we must do so that the new life you seek becomes a possibility. The hour is close, and I must depart. I have long anticipated this moment, and the time for change is now. Throughout all of our rich and long history, Calderont was ruled by kings and queens of great stature. We felt that only those who proved themselves through heroic deeds and great magnanimity toward the people should rule. There was no line of succession to ensure this. Each generation had to produce a king and queen who could perpetuate the continued prosperity and goodwill of our people. Now that chain is broken because I must leave and my beloved father has paid a terrible price for ridding us of our greatest scourge, the Dragon of Maladour.

"This is what I propose based on your own wishes and the pledge of loyalty you extended to our way of life. I will convene a Council for Unity made up of your leadership, Pentamon from the Circle of the Wise, and my father, noble King Salasand. Your mission will be to conduct the affairs of our state with an eye toward that which is of benefit to you all. You will need special skill to do that, and none is wiser than Pentamon and my father to guide you in this. Otherwise you will degenerate into faction and intrigue, which marked the world you left. Embrace your unity, for in that all is possible. Without it nothing will stand and catastrophe will surely seek you out. Treat each other as if you all shared one bloodline. When a nation promotes kinship in all its citizens, it becomes a realm of kindness and civility. No one will seek advantage over his brother or sister, and the least among you will be tended to first. Don't fear growth or change.

"Most of all discover and recreate the beauty that is around you. Our forebears knew that a land rich in gardens, parks, and fountains and a people with great respect for the creatures of the forest would have no appetite for war. Continue the beautification of Calderont. Your children will celebrate that even more than you because they are closer to that state from whence we all came. And when you deliberate, assemble in the Hall of the Covenant. It is the place of your transformation, and it will keep you solemn and to the task."

Many of the tribal people wept at the possibility. All had dreamt of a world such as this, but not one leader from the realm of power and acquisition could or would create it. The Calderi for their part would have to adjust to a new way of governance, but they had the foresight to realize that Chrysallia was affording them the only opportunity to continue their way of life. She had converted these "vascistes," and now they were as committed to the well-being of Calderont as were its most revered citizens. From this day forward, the denigrating term "vasciste" was never used again.

Chrysallia invited her father to speak so that all could benefit from his wisdom and insight. He had to be helped to his feet, for his legs were without the strength of his youth. Yet his voice was loud and confident. He surveyed the congregation of the Calderi and the tribal people, and he was glad. When they sat and became silent, he spoke: "Citizens of Calderont, old and new, opportunity of the greatest import lies before you. I have always believed that we are all called to a destiny and that change occurs without accident but of necessity and out of design. My fate was to rid the land of the Dragon of Maladour. This I have done, but I have paid a price. I am unable to rule. To some that is not only my tragedy but a tragedy for all in the realm. I have learned otherwise. There is a reason, just as there was a reason why good King Althius did not kill the dragon himself. I have long suspected that in his youth, he had to kill a dragon of a different sort, because that is how a king or queen rises to full stature. A void is created that must be filled, and he or she who comes forth discovers his or her full measure as each faces that which has not yet been tasted. Once that journey begins, once the threshold is crossed, the magic of discovery begins.

"King Althius had to find a successor. He would know who that successor was only when the dragon came. For only a dragon slayer can become king or queen. You may not see the dragons, but they are there. They will always be there calling you to greatness, and greatness will not find you without them. When I accomplished the deed, King Althius knew.

"A new void has been created today. It must be filled by my daughter who must leave and by you who must stay to do what you have never done—rule. Many will say you are not ready, that the pitfalls are too great, that the unity you have been called to foster has never worked in all of history. You of the tribes have come from a world where survival hinges on killing your enemies and converting them to be like you. And what you have discovered is a history where there is no end to enemies because the values you embrace create new ones every day.

"The world turns on what a man sees when he opens his eyes. If he sees that which he fears, conflict will be his universe. But if he sees his brother and sister, a new world forms in the blink of his eye. You are called to fill a void, to do what has never been done. If you succeed, this place and a thousand more like it will blossom. I am crippled for a reason—so that you may walk."

There was a long ribbon of silence as the wise Salasand sat. His words hung in the air and washed over the assemblage as if they had experienced an anointing. As one they rose and chanted his name in ever-increasing decibels because they saw the road to the future they all sought. Good Salasand was the sign post pointing the way.

And then all grew silent. The moment for all that was to begin had arrived. Chrysallia, unarmed and but fifteen years, was to cross the portal that could be the beginning or end to their world. She embraced her father for the last time, took her farewell from the people, and left behind the childhood she so loved forever.

CHAPTER 6:
SPIRITS OF FENDOR

Chrysallia, for all her determination, was alone for the first time in her life. The impulse to turn around and run back was overwhelming. Yet the obligation to her people and the nobility in her veins steeled her for the journey, and she pressed forward.

With the early morning sun at her back, she followed the timeworn descent to the waterfall that led to the thresholds of Fendor. She had always relished those trips to the forest floor with her father or playmates to sit in silence and watch for hours the crash of water undeterred by the sullen rocks interrupting its course as it hit the pool awaiting its descent. Time was suspended in those moments of delight with the roar and gurgle of cascading water fed by the conjoining of rivulets that bisected Calderont as the land sloped to confront the mouth of the waiting forest below. Her senses were continuously provoked by the intoxicating scent of the purple sarquella blooms, in the sight of the multiple rainbows that formed through the mist as the sun protruded through the droplets rebounding from the stony projections at the rim of the pool. She was always enchanted by the play of the deer that came to the salt licks that lined the brooks emanating from the far end of the basin. Luminescent butterflies also came to the licks, and it always enchanted her that they would alight on her nose or forehead as if she too had nectar to feed their cravings.

She followed the stream at the far end of the pool as it dropped in a slow rush from the overspill of its banks. Tracking its course for several miles, she was alarmed when it disappeared over a precipice of several hundred feet and she could no longer use it to navigate. Then the forest rose up before her as the sun disappeared in a cluster of clouds. The trees grew thick, and there was no discernible path for entry. A slow panic gnawed at her. She could still find her way home now by just turning around and retracing the stream to the waterfall.

Remembering her father's initiation into the woods of Maladour, she knew this was the only course for her as well. She espied a small breach in the phalanx of trees and entered. The forest was alive with the cacophony of bird trills, the chatter of squirrels, and the buzzing of insects. The air had been dry and crisp along the sparse vegetation around the stream. Now it grew dense and humid. She had to be careful of her footing as the slowly rising elevation was pocked with moss-covered rock and fallen trees. The ground at her feet was thick with matted leaves and pine needles, forcing her eyes to the forest floor to secure her footing.

These woods had instruction for those who could see, she mused, for all around her were dead trunks of fallen boughs rotting in the moist forest air. But out of that decay, saplings were profusely taking their place. The insects fed off the dead bark, and all manner of creatures made their living devouring the grubs that grew fat from this cellulose feast. And the forest floor became enriched by the compost left from these droppings. Ferns decorated the many embankments where erosion was prevented by the roots that grabbed the rush of rain water. Laurels and a myriad of forest flowers were the by-products of this process. It was as if the forest knew that death was the mother of beauty. The decay was actually fueling its rebirth. She could see it. It was as if the forest controlled its own destiny. Nothing was wasted, and the cycle of life, death, and resurrection had been unbroken for eons.

All of a sudden the chatter stopped, and the only sound she heard was her own feet treading on the fallen leaves. It grew dark. For the first time she looked up. The trees were majestic, but they blocked the sun enough to allow the minimum light necessary to sustain life on the ever-changing forest floor. It was just past midday, yet it seemed as if dusk had already descended. The humidity made her uncomfortable, and her clothes began to stick to her skin from her sweat. The air was also fat from the resin of evergreens that thrived in this climate. It must have rained the night before, for the scent of them suffused the forest.

Chrysallia thought she heard a rustling. She froze. Her eyes darted in every direction until she espied a chipmunk chirping at her for intruding on his daily forage. The play of scant sunlight that penetrated the canopy and mingled with the shadows cast by these giant, leafy sentinels made it difficult to distinguish any form of animation.

She heard rustling again and halted in her tracks. This time there was no chipmunk. Her pulse quickened. She scanned the panorama of light and shade, leaf and needle, bark and mulch, fern and fungus. Nothing.

Then she froze in horror. Not fifty feet in front of her, crouched as if to pounce, was a huge spotted cat with penetrating, intense green eyes. Its fur was a grayish white pocked with black rosettes so that it was barely distinguishable no matter the time of day. It blended in perfectly with the diffused light on the forest floor.

She was paralyzed. It was as if the cat had hypnotized her with its fiery glance. Its tail twitched as it took its measure of the distance between them, and before Chrysallia could turn to run, it was on her. Knocked to the ground by a swipe of the beast's giant paw, she awaited the bite to the neck and the expiration of life.

A long second passed. Then another. She was not hurt, but she was too afraid to look up. The cat pawed at her as if in some dark play before the bite to the throat. But the bite never came. The cat nuzzled her and then lay on its back to reveal its beautiful underbelly of white fur.

Chrysallia remembered the wolf that had greeted her father and guided him to the Tor of Magadorn. She also recalled the many times Salasand told her that the totem would come when the threshold was breached. Hers had arrived, a creature of black and white, life and death. And then another epiphany. The stuffed cat creature that had accompanied her to bed all her childhood days may have found animation here again to guide her in her quest.

She scratched the cat's belly where it met its ribs, and the beast purred a low growl of contentment. Chrysallia was enthralled at the beauty of this creature. She petted it incessantly, and it rubbed up against her legs and marked her with the scent glands in its face. They were lost in the play of mutual discovery unique to the love that occurs between man and beast.

"You shall have a name," she chimed. "I will call you Salasar the Magnificent. What do you think of that?" The beast eyed her playfully and roared its approval.

Night fell quickly, and Salasar guided her to a forest rill where the water was cold and pure. A profusion of berries and forest fruits abounded, and Chrysallia ate and drank her fill. Then Salasar went off to hunt. As daylight stole its way through the breaks in the boughs at the forest canopy, Chrysallia saw Salasar's maw covered in blood. It had killed and was fastidiously cleaning itself oblivious to the horror in Chrysallia's face. How could a creature so beautiful be so fierce at the same time? She wondered.

As Salasar caught her glance, it approached her with what seemed like a purpose. It bounded a few feet and then turned as if beckoning her to follow. Chrysallia knew. Salasar would deliver her to her destiny.

They trekked the entire day past glades and glens with Salasar always in front guiding the course. By dusk they had arrived at a modest hut nestled in a break in the tree line hard by a stream. Salasar sat on its haunches and roared. A form emerged that looked like the melding of a man and a tree. He was tall, gaunt, and droop eyed, as if in a state of perpetual sadness. His hair was crowned with twigs, tendrils, and flowers that marked him as monarch of this sylvan realm. His long, bony fingers looked like branchy appendages and his body was covered with hair resembling matted pine needles. There was no way of telling his age, but his face resembled the texture of ancient beech trees.

He greeted Salasar with affection. "What have you brought me today, old friend?"

Chrysallia replied, "I am Princess Chrysallia, daughter of Salasand the Dragon Slayer and Beldonia the Merciful. I seek your hospitality and guidance, for I must reach the land of the despoilers who are threatening the way of life of the Calderi people."

The gaunt forest creature intoned, "I am Drougen, guardian of Fendor. I know well the Calderi, for they enter the borders of my realm with reverence for my creatures and trees. They replace what they take and have found peace from the secrets hidden in the seasons of the forest. But the people you speak of are the curse of all that is pure and untouched. They destroy the ancient trees. They have machines that foul the air. The rains laden with their fumes burn all manner of vegetation. They stalk my creatures for sport almost to their extinction.

"What they do not know is that the forest will have its revenge when all is gone. Their air will boil, their cities will flood, and they will compete for what is left until they utterly annihilate themselves.

"Yet there are forces here in Fendor that you will encounter that can kill them all now. You have much to discover and much to learn for so young a child. There is a possibility you can reclaim them. But not until you reclaim yourself. Come and rest. I will prepare your meal and give you a good bed to sleep in this night."

Chrysallia paid him obeisance and was eager to begin her tutelage. But it did not come as she anticipated, and it would not come from the spoken word.

CHAPTER 7:
CHRYSALLIA'S DREAM

That night Drougen prepared an appetizing stew made of legumes, roots, and mushrooms. Chrysallia ate heartily and was glad for the shelter as well. As was its wont, Salasar left to hunt, and it was better for Chrysallia not to see the creature she so loved show its bloodlust and ferocity, for it could not consume a meal without violence. The duality of this beast fascinated her. It was black and white, loving and ferocious, and yet the two streams were in perfect harmony in the cat. Its inner dynamic was without conflict. She pondered whether there was some hidden message in this.

While the forest guardian's accommodations were rustic, his wooden chairs and bed were sturdy and comfortable. He had a potpourri of dried flowers and pinecones in a clay bowl on his table, and the scent of evergreen resin, though subtle, pleased her senses. She grew tired and then dizzy. When she lay down on the bed of Drougen, the room immediately began to tremble, and she fell into a panic. For the first time in her life she had lost control. Pulse racing and in a sweat, her last thought before plummeting into a delirium was that Drougen had poisoned her. Then all manner of light evaporated as she swooned into a realm more magical than even the Forest of Fendor.

A new journey had begun. Chrysallia found herself in front of a massive tree so broad it was like a forest itself. When she turned to face it, the darkness was impenetrable. And from some point beyond her ken, a form began to loom out of its bowels. To her horror she saw that it was Viladon himself holding his severed head. "You must die," the head bellowed.

Chrysallia recoiled in stony horror. For a moment she could not move or speak. Although her face was contorted in sheer panic, no sound passed her lips. Collecting her senses, she felt the blood return to her legs. She fled the head and fled the darkness, more terrified than at any other time in her life. The more she ran, the more the darkness lifted.

Soon with some distance between her and the tree, she grew calm. Of a sudden the sun shone brilliantly, and the air was crisp and dry. From afar she espied an old man, bald and grave, coming toward her carrying a shepherd's staff. He was walking toward the tree. As their paths met, she awaited his greeting, but none was forthcoming. He stared at her sadly, seemed inclined to say something, and then just nodded and continued his journey toward the dark abyss she was seeking to escape. She followed his steady gait for a few moments, turned, and pushed on in her own direction. The scene grew increasingly pleasant.

To her amusement a troop of eight young boys all dressed in white came upon her. Unlike the old man, they immediately shouted a greeting and engaged her in play. Their exuberance and laughter brought her much delight. She felt a deep urge to remain in their company. They all grabbed hands to begin a circle dance moving in a counterclockwise direction. She thought they should be going the opposite way, but the last boy grabbed her wrist and pulled her into their ring.

At the first turn she saw an enchanting sight. Not more than a half league away was a walled expanse bisected by a gigantic and decorous iron gate. She let go of the hand that held her wrist and was compulsively drawn to this idyllic spot. The children followed her. As she examined the filigree and swirl of the ironwork, she was mesmerized by the representations of youth not much older than herself in various forms of embrace. Emotions never previously felt began to pulse and stir within her. She was fascinated. It was as if the depictions of amorous frolic triggered that which had long been incubating within her. She remembered her mother's warm response to her girlish inquisitions about love and matters of the heart. The good Queen Beldonia told her she would know when the moment came. Most of all she said she could learn of love from those who were in love.

Chrysallia didn't have to look far. She had always relished the intimacy of her parents. She would see them enrapt in conversation or compulsively caressing one another. Her father was forever surprising his queen with flowers and little gifts, and Beldonia in turn showered him with an affection of which he never grew tired. Knowing she was the product of such profound engagement made her feel good and special.

"Maybe such a delight awaits me on the other side," she wondered. The enticement was visceral, for there beyond the grated portal was an estate like no other. Expanses of perfectly trimmed lawn were accentuated by elevated rock gardens pocked with miniscule lichens, moss, and periwinkle. Weeping trees of red feathery leaf were at their crests, and the rocks were moist from the trickle of the rillets that gently cascaded over their stony façades. At the center of this elegant panorama was a fountain framed with boxwood and fed by these healing waters, which displaced a pool several feet deep. And there as if rising from a point below the surface was a statue of a young water god carrying a captivating nymph toward the waiting lawn.

Chrysallia was enchanted. She longed to go through the gate, but there was no opening through which to enter. The next thing she knew she had passed right through the bars. Delighted, she raced toward the fountain. The little boys tried to follow, but they were not allowed. Staring through the latticework, they watched Chrysallia enter the beckoning waters. She was aroused by the musk of the boxwood and the play of diamond-flickering sunlight shimmering on the surface of the pool. She had to see the faces of these young lovers whose eyes knew no other distraction.

As she waded knee-deep toward their marbled embrace, she happened to look down at the bottom of the fountain. Little black globules were rising to the surface. They were disgusting, she thought. Her revulsion and frustration at having so aesthetic a scene interrupted quickly turned to the same horror she had faced at the tree. The globules turned into an inky whirlpool as the bottom of the pool seemed to capsize, drawing all the water to an unseen chasm far below. Chrysallia could not escape. She was sucked down into the maelstrom unable to breathe. Viladon was right. She was going to die. Her breath left her for a moment, but in that same instance she found herself back at the tree, only this time she was playing in its branches.

When she awoke, there was Drougen quietly mopping her sweated brow. Startled, she jumped up and angrily confronted him. "Did you poison me with that potion?"

Drougen knowingly responded, "The mushrooms and tubers of this forest are powerful stimulants. They can provide transport to the uncharted realms deep within where different and profound truths abide. I have long known that words are without value for those whose answers lie beyond that which is printed by men. So it is with you."

Chrysallia understood, but what answers could she obtain from an experience outside the measure of her own reasoning? She quickly recounted her dream to him, careful not to leave out even a single detail. He listened and nodded knowingly. "What does it mean?" she pleaded. "Am I going to die? Why was Viladon gone when I got back to the tree? Why didn't the old man speak to me? Why were the little boys wearing white, and why weren't they allowed to come with me past the gate?"

Drougen put his head down for a moment and then faced her. "If I tell you the full meaning of the dream, you will miss the trials you must undergo to truly understand what the Spirit Force is transmitting to you. What is clear is that the darkness you feared at the tree had to be confronted no matter how much you tried to avoid it. Your journey ultimately took you to the whirlpool, where you surely thought you would meet your end. That didn't happen. You not only lived, but after your immersion into the waters, you rose up to not only face the tree but also play in its branches.

"That is all I can tell you. The rest will come before you leave this forest and before you set foot on the land of those you must transform. And you will not be able to move or motivate them with violence or threats. This you must learn and the forest will provide your instruction. I am always here and in many forms, but if you need to find me, know that I will come to you."

Just then the sun opened its sleep-laden eyes to splash the first rays of light on the bloody maw of Salasar, who had just returned to the hovel after feasting mightily while Chrysallia was lost in reverie. Slaking its thirst in the brook behind Drougen's modest quarters, it turned to Chrysallia and roared its intent. It was time to leave.

CHAPTER 8:
THE FIRE WITHIN

Fendor was full of mystery, danger, and delight. It spanned a multitude of geologic zones from barren volcanic wastelands, to meadows rich for grazing, to mountains of mist and forest, to semiarid dry beds where only snakes and scorpions abounded. But none was richer in glade and all manner of vegetation than the lake region near its eastern rim. It was to this spot that Salasar escorted her.

Unlike her initial foray, Chrysallia found the forest here invigorating and pleasant. She could hear the murmur of brooks coursing through the silent wood that drank its fill from the watery gift at its feet. The expanses between the numerous lakes and ponds fed by these mountain streams opened to vistas of grassy plains where the antlered and horned beasts of the forest fed. In the sun-drenched meadows they frolicked, fought for supremacy, and mated. Here too were the predators that fattened their young on the bounty of horn and hoof that were exposed in the open expanses.

By midday they neared a small lake of no more than several hundred yards at its farthest reach. Its banks were lined with all manner of reeds and interspersed with orange, white, and maroon daylilies. Many of the lake-lined trees were of weeping habit so their lowest limbs almost reached their own shimmering reflections that gently wafted on the glassy surface with every gentle breeze. Two swans claimed the pool as their own and silently glided across its stillness only to disappear neck first in the shallows as they feasted on the vegetation at the lake bed below. The fallen limbs near the embankments provided haven for the turtles that came to bask in the heat of the afternoon sun. Frogs fed voraciously on the larva of insects and any bug foolhardy to come within striking distance of their lashing tongues. Colorful fish congregated to feed in the small coves where schools of their smaller cousins swirled in avoidance.

The drama of life and death could be seen even to the depths, for the water was clear from the filtering vegetation that removed the debris transported by the rushing brooks that fed the lake. At its farthest end where the tall trees stood as sentries protecting the privacy of this pristine interlude was an inviting hut nestled in the lower branches of an immense gray-barked beech where the boughs were thickest for support. Salasar spotted a motion in the canopy and shrunk in a stalking pose. Something was sporting in the treetops.

Before Chrysallia could even blink, Salasar exploded in a rush to the tree. In a trice she was flying in chase through the dense branches and vines, and Chrysallia was horrified that she would witness this spotted guardian that she so loved kill an innocent creature in a bloodlust. Before she could blink, Salasar emitted a roar of triumph as she reached her quarry. In a leap of extraordinary distance she brought her prey down, and both hit the water in a flourish.

When they emerged, Chrysallia was spellbound. Rising from the depths was the most compelling youth she had ever seen. He swam rapidly to the shore to escape the fatal jaws of the most dangerous feline in the forest. He was tall, over six feet, with a sinewy and well-defined musculature. His face was the comeliest she had ever seen. While not yet sporting the rubble of one more mature, his cheekbones were high on his face, eyes large and piercing, and his lips were as full as freshly cut figs. His hair glistened in the sunlight as he shook it to release the drench from his plunge. It fell to his shoulders. His skin was bronze and stood in contrast to his perfectly formed white teeth that smiled through parting lips as he espied her. His loins were barely covered in a pelt as he faced her trembling form. But it was too late. Before he could continue his escape, Salasar was on him. Chrysallia froze in horror. How could the most beautiful youth she had ever seen be killed by the spotted panther she had come to love?

The boy twisted from Salasar's embrace, got behind her, arm around her head, and seemed to whisper to her. The cat sprang loose and knocked him down. The boy grabbed her by the face as she stood over him, and they wrestled in this manner for what seemed like hours. He could have been her cub, Chrysallia thought. They were tireless as they teased each other in a frolic that was clearly repeated often in their relationship.

Finally Salasar calmed, and the boy beckoned Chrysallia to join them on the far end of the lake by the hut. She had to swim because her path was blocked by moss-covered boulder outcrops that could not be traversed. The water was warm in the shallows, but as she reached the middle expanse where the pool was at its greatest depth, it got progressively colder.

The boy disappeared in a blink, and the next thing she knew he emerged from the depths to lift her in his arms to bring her to the far shore. She almost fell in a swoon at the strength of him, and the touch of his skin, smooth and sensuous, awakened appetites dormant in her to this moment. She was enthralled and her breath became short in his caress.

Salasar seemed to approve as she rubbed against them both. They were amazed at the power of her tail as it almost knocked them over while she pivoted to repeat her marking of them as her own. The day was spent coursing through the treetops and exploring the lakeside to partake of its delights. The boy came upon a stand of sarquella blooms and quickly fastened them into a tiara for her to wear as queen of the watery domain that was once exclusively his. He fed her exotic fruits and played on a lute he fashioned from a turtle shell. Time abandoned them both as the air, fat with the fading sunlight and rich in the perfume of exotic lilies and aromatic sarquellas gave them pause to glance across the lake as the two swans left the water to roost.

And then they faced each other. Both seemed drunk from overindulgence in the sights and smells of this panorama of sensory delight. They could not escape each other's gaze. She played with his hair. He sang to her. The sun began to set behind two youths on their way to becoming lovers.

He took her to his hut, and there on his bed of down and hide they reclined. Soon both were asleep, exhausted from exploring a world as if experienced for the first time, because lovers always rediscover that which is lost to the eyes when alone.

Around midnight she awoke. There before her was the form that fired her passions as nothing before and probably after, she thought. Impulsively she began to trace with her hand the contour of his face, the rich curve of his lips and brows, the cheeks flushed in sleep from the image of her enshrined in his dream, the rise of his breast and the nub of his nipples. His torso, even in repose, was ribbed, and she could feel that tautness even in his slumber. His legs were defined but smooth.

As she returned to his face, she touched his lips. She felt herself trembling as if a thousand doves were beating within her breast seeking exit and release. She raised herself so that she could kiss him. As her face neared the source of her desire, she realized she would never leave his side, ever. He awoke to see her own rich lips nearing his awaiting kiss. His hands reached to pull her on top of him. She couldn't resist-her body on fire at the feast of him.

Of a sudden a light seemed to flicker faintly across his face. It grew in scope until it filled the space to the point where his bed high in the treetops was illuminated. She rose and walked to the entrance of his hut still trembling with desire. There, just above the entrance, fireflies were swarming, and like a beacon they revealed what the unseen eye missed. A shape was being formed. It was the Sword of Salasand, and in that moment, Chrysallia knew that her physical desires were strong enough to pull the purpose from her quest; that her passions were the soft, enticing dragon no less dangerous in stealing from her the object of her odyssey than the dragon of fear in never allowing the journey to begin in the first place.

Without hesitation she dove into the cold waters of the lake and swam to the nearest shore where Salasar was waiting. The big cat curled around the still-shaking Chrysallia and gave her warmth. In the embrace of this beast she knew she was back on her path and a test had been passed. Before she fell asleep, her dream flashed before her. She saw the fountain and the two sculptures in embrace, and she knew. Her father's words echoed over her exhausted form: "A real hero conquers himself before conquering his dragon." This she had done. "When my task is complete," she mused, "I will find him again and claim him for my own." Spent from her physical and emotional ordeal, she quickly fell asleep, but no images interrupted her slumber.

CHAPTER 9:
ꟼNDOLENCE

ꟼn the morning, Chrysallia rose and wistfully looked at the now abandoned hut where she almost tasted for the first time the love she knew had engulfed her parents all their lives. "No wonder my father was so forlorn at my mother's passing," she groused. "I have not even sampled what he celebrated through all his years, and I am in mourning from a loss I may never replace."

Salasar sensed her mood, wheeled, and got between her and the seat of her desire. She cuffed Chrysallia as she would a recalcitrant cub that would not follow. Taking her final glance at what could have been, Chrysallia turned and trailed the all-knowing Salasar, who was already leading her on the path to the next trial awaiting the Princess of Possibility, the name she would be called through the ages.

The enchanting land of streams and lakes slowly receded from sight as the two reached higher ground. Periodically Salasar paused as if straining to smell or hear that which she was seeking. Chrysallia heard nothing, but she was growing tired in the thin air just below the tree line of the mountain that her spotted guardian was traversing. There were chasms and gorges that regularly interrupted their path. The clouds hung low around the precipitous drops, and at times they could barely see through the dense mist. These were not the highest of peaks in Fendor, but they certainly were the most remote and the most dangerous.

Any traveler unescorted would have easily fallen to his death unaware that his next step was his last. Salasar made sure that Chrysallia had her hand on her tail because the cloud cover made navigation impossible to the naked eye. One could not even see his foot much less the path being trod. No matter the promise enshrined in these peaks, no one could safely find the way in or out, except for Salasar.

The wind carried a faint lilt that could have been dismissed as the cooing of doves or the caroling of songbirds that frequented these mountain haunts during the nesting season. The upper ranges offered little sustenance for predators of the eggs now incubating under the down of their feathered parents who artfully crafted their nests into the smallest of crevices—inaccessible until the fledglings molted their baby feathers and were ready to fly. The skrill of raptors occasionally broke the muffled songbirds' rapture as they impaled an unsuspecting chick trying its wings for the first time.

After another hour's climb, Chrysallia heard the lilting grow increasingly amplified, and as the cloud cover broke, she clearly heard the unmistakable refrains of children singing. "How could anyone live in such a forbidding clime?" she wondered and dismissed the possibility to the tricks played on the senses in such rarefied air. But singing it was, often followed by traces of laughter common to the play of excited boys and girls lost in their games and rituals of discovery.

It was mesmerizing to Chrysallia, and the association unleashed a store of memories of days given to unceasing joy as she and her mates romped through the parks and greens of the Calderont of her youth. She grew pensive, but not for long. For there, spanning a cavernous drop to the solitary mountain facing her was a bridge like no other she had ever seen. Barely wide enough for one person to cross, its base was made of hemp that did not afford much footing. Salasar stopped at the base and left her.

Chrysallia felt as she had when she first entered Fendor. Part of her wanted to retreat and follow Salasar to another destiny, but the cat was gone. As she turned back to face the abyss looming in front of her, there on the other side of the bridge was a little boy dressed in white beckoning her to cross. A new world was waiting and a new challenge to her will in a realm that would seem all too familiar.

Refusing to look down, Chrysallia trembled with each halting step until she reached the smiling face of the child awaiting her. He was not surprised by her presence and gave greeting as if she were the playmate he was expecting. Taking her hand, he led her to the chorus of laughter and rhyme emanating from just beyond the bend of the road at the base of the bridge.

What mystical place is this, she wondered, for all manner of sprites were darting past her laden with honeycombs, candied fruits, and toys of every size and appeal. As she turned beyond the last stand of trees blocking her view, there before her was a formidable gate. It was opened invitingly to let her in, and the most delightful little village she had ever seen was alive with the bustle of little boys and girls at play. The houses were miniature in size and decorated with furniture customized for the occupants within. There were chairs and wooden beds laden with dolls, stuffed creatures of the forests, and icons of heroes and heroines who inspired the imagination of these little celebrants safely ensconced in the world of mirth. The import of their quests and journeys were known only to them. All were given names, and though they were made of stuffing and marbles, to the children who animated them they were as alive as the puppies and kittens who cavorted endlessly with each and every one of them.

Chrysallia could not stop laughing at their exuberance. The weather within the gated compound was perfect, and there were mudslides, wading pools, and playgrounds in abundance depending on the whim of the group as to the venue of their choosing. And the sprites seemed to be everywhere. They were the cooks, handmaidens, nurses, and cleaning service that the children required, for the little imps were without any responsibility whatsoever. There was no formal time to retire either, but the minute darkness fell, all were safely nestled within their quaint abodes, and that's when Chrysallia came upon a startling discovery. Their parents would appear at bedtime to dress them in their nightclothes, shower them with affection, and tell them a tale about the stuffed figures that were the basis of their childhood mythologies.

When the tykes grew tired, the torches were lit so the darkness could not harbor the ogres and dark spirits that grew powerful and dangerous in the absence of light. All the doors to all the bedrooms were always left slightly ajar so if a nightmare became real, escape was possible. The parents would never leave the house so the streets, yards, and greens were exclusive to the little people who inhabited this magical commune.

Chrysallia was the celebrity of this kingdom. Every day they swarmed over her and begged for stories or companionship in play. This proved irresistible to her, and with each activity she became more like them. Soon it was time for her to have her own cottage, and with great fanfare she was led to a larger accommodation with a decorous white fence that framed a modest flower garden. The path to the door was of white stone as well. On the portal, a wreath of dried flowers was neatly hung, guarded by two large toy soldiers. There was a birdbath at the center of her front yard that was the hub of activity every morning. Their chirping as they bathed and cleaned their feathers was the signal that playtime was at hand, and that's when the village began to stir.

Inside her cottage, the walls were brightly painted with scenes from her own salad days in Calderont. The dolls and stuffed creatures that accompanied her to the land of her dreams were lined upon her bed, and the cupboard was replete with all her favorite treats, and her requisite bedtime companion, the guardian cat, took the prominent position at her pillow. Chrysallia was at peace, for she was loved and needed, child and mother, the princess of a domain of innocence, joy, and tranquility. In time she lost all ambition as the routine of play and nurturing filled her days. The world beyond the gate with all its misery and conflict was a forgotten memory. For her it ceased to exist. This was home.

One day, as she was lost in a game of search and discover, Chrysallia hid just beyond the bend leading to the village. They would never find her here, she thought, for the children were loath to go anywhere near the gate or the path leading from it. It was not a conscious fear, for nothing intruded on the mindset of these young phantoms of frivolity. But when one was brave enough to go beyond the curve in the road, she would pounce on the unsuspecting naïf and tickle him just to hear that gasp of delicious shock as she found the spot that would unleash the spasm of laughter she loved to hear.

While she lay in wait, she heard a great buzzing from across the span beyond the gate. There was smoke rising far on the horizon, and as the wind took a turn in her direction, an echo of what sounded like shouts and screams reached her. She exited the giant portal to investigate. There across the bridge was Salasar puling the way great cats do when calling their young. The world had just intruded on the innocence to which she had retreated.

Chrysallia froze. And then a resounding clang was heard as the great gate closed with finality on the child who dared to leave the protection and security that was promised to those who stayed on the safe side of life. Her epiphany was attenuated when she saw eight little boys dressed in white waving farewell once again because it was not their time to leave their kingdom, and it was painfully clear to Chrysallia that she could never retreat from that which she had to face no matter the promise. Her eyes welled with tears as she waved her farewell to her yet untested charges. She wept for the violations she knew they would incur, and she wept not for her lost youth but for the longing in her to bear children such as these. She had become a woman.

CHAPTER 10:
THE DRAGON WITHIN

The Princess of Possibility was now steeled in the awareness of how indolence can sap the will and block any thought of movement or responsibility. And it could do it by playing to the mind's need for contentment, which always has its provenience in childhood. Yet it was also clear to her that the purity and spontaneity of one's early years should abide through adult life. These are the things that make life worth living, she concluded, and these are the reasons why we love to be in the company of children. We delight in their honesty and unfiltered response to life. This was affirmed in her.

She faced the world that called her to task and traversed the span leading to Salasar. The guardian cat immediately welcomed her, and Chrysallia threw her arms around her neck in loving embrace. She pulled back to look at this magnificent creature. "Who is she?" Chrysallia mused. "She knows every realm and every spirit in Fendor." What she didn't know was that the answer to her question would be revealed when her quest was complete.

What also began to percolate within Chrysallia was the fact that there was wisdom beyond words and that initiation was the only true teacher. "Enlightenment can never come from the word," she reflected. "That was the problem with these priests," she reasoned. They relied on vocabulary to access the spirit world when it was in fact vocabulary that prevented the mystical experience they craved. To her mind, more could be learned about the suffusing force of life by lying on one's back and experiencing the endless expanse of sky and star than all that was written in the texts of men. This she would have to confront–and soon.

Chrysallia, however, was in no position to make pronouncements about the limitations of others because she was not yet the initiate she would become. Salasar gave her an impatient glare as if to underscore there was more to follow. With a low purr she turned and led Chrysallia in the direction of the smoke at the far end of Fendor.

The final trek to the backlands of Fendor was arduous, for they were forced to take the circuitous route around the Galamore chain, and this forced them to traverse numerous rapids and dense forests to reach the boundaries of this mystical wood. On the way they saw evidence of the flight from the kingdoms Chrysallia would have to engage, for there were decomposing bodies of the unfortunates who had either succumbed to starvation, fatigue, or attack by the beasts whose land they had violated.

At last they reached the final bastion of the Galamore chain, and the height from this last peak gave them their first view of the six kingdoms whose dark history was a blight to their own world and a threat to the realm of Calderont. The panorama was revealing. The forests on the façade of the mountain facing their domains were almost stripped bare. There were crops cut into the soil, but also evidence that mudslides and flood had wrecked most of that because the natural vegetation held back the erosion. This was no longer the case, and the mindless exploitation of the source of their well-being, the renewing and enriching forest, continued apace. If left unchecked, all would end within a hundred years.

Just then Chrysallia heard the deafening buzz that had broken her concentration during the game of discovery by the portal of the Village of the Innocent from whence she came. Turning, she saw what appeared to be a monstrous, stinging insect with wings so powerful they kicked up dust in great whirls as the creature neared the ground. Yet there was something distinctly human about it too, for it spoke to her when it finally alit a few yards from where she was standing.

"I am Garantapede, lord of the Drones, sent to protect the lands of Fendor from the malefactors. I have learned of your coming from the wise Drougen who tells me you are on a quest to convert the rulers of the six kingdoms to do what they have refused to do for two millennia. Let me prove to you the futility of such a course. Climb on my back, and I will show you their destructive legacy."

Chrysallia obeyed, for she knew she would need an understanding of the forces driving their world to its dark destiny. She affixed her legs around Garantapede's pinched waist and held on to the two antennae projecting from his head.

Leaving an eddy of ground debris in their wake, they left the earthly confine and soared at great speed over the expanse below. Chrysallia was exhilarated at the rush of wind in her face and the speed of this powerful monarch of Fendor's skies as it darted to its destinations. What she saw quickly dispelled any thrill from this excursion. There below, she saw belches of smoke from all manner of engines penetrating the pristine air above them. The habitats of this race were compressed with multitudes to such an extent that there were never enough resources just to feed them. In such tight proximity the people were prone to violence. Chrysallia could see the needy and old living aimlessly on streets, ignored as if they never existed. She saw magnificent places of worship within their midst as if the buildings had more value than the neglected souls beyond it. Near their borders were streams of refugees going from one misery to another, for they were never welcome wherever they went.

And when Garantapede reached the so-called sacred places, there was more violence one toward the other there than at any other venue. It was as if the one thing that they declared was moral and good became the justification for indiscriminate slaughter because of a few paragraphs of disagreement in each of their sacred texts. She could see the pulpits where their priests and so-called holy men preached either destruction of nonbelievers or violence of another sort—that the chosen, which all factions were convinced were themselves, were superior and uniquely invested in salvation. The rest would discover the errors of their ways when they died only to reawaken to damnation and exile.

Their lands were crowded with machines that were supposed to provide them with leisure and cultural pursuits, but that outcome was never realized.

The people became more mechanical and less feeling the wealthier they got. And their progress came at a terrible price. Floods, cataclysmic weather systems, and the disappearance of habitat were the inevitable by-products of such mindless pursuits. The welter of conflict, persecution, pollution, and indifference sickened Chrysallia, and Garantapede, sensing she had seen enough, returned to the peak where she first surveyed this dismal scene.

When they alit, Garantapede spoke. "These people will never change, and at this point even if they did, the damage they have done is irreversible. They are doomed. If we can hasten the process, we may yet save our world."

Chrysallia was still wavering. Garantapede saw his chance and spoke again. "You are thinking that there are many who are innocent and helpless in this dark endeavor. That is a viewpoint that their own ethical systems might embrace. But we are forces of the earth. If multitudes of them perished, including what you call the good along with the bad, this earth would let out a sigh of relief just from the removal of the weight of them. And if all of them perished, Calderont, Zod, Fendor, and Maladour live. It is your choice, for I will assemble at your disposal my army, which I can assure you will destroy them utterly."

Garantapede's voice and tone changed as if some secret code was being employed, and in seconds the forests and skies above Fendor were vibrating from the thunderous gathering of hordes of Garantapede's army who were almost identical in appearance to him. They gathered in squadrons to the left and right of Chrysallia. The sound of those wings in vicious flutter got her blood up. From their abdomens protruded curved scimitars filled with venom. There would be no recovery from any cut or piercing visited upon the enemy from even the slightest puncture. She finally had the power to protect her world, and she would use it.

She howled in hatred at the land below: "I will break you now utterly for the vermin that you are." Mounting Garantapede, whose eyes took on a reddish glow in rage and hate, she intoned, "At my signal, unleash your troops and kill them all." All she had to do was drop her hand, and the deadly storm would descend upon the unsuspecting populations below. In a second it would be done.

Chrysallia could not hear the roar of caution from Salasar, for in that moment mounted on a drone next to her appeared Viladon. Instead of brandishing his own head, he held suspended in his hands the head of her mother, Queen Beldonia.

Chrysallia shrieked in horror. She was a hair from repeating her father's tragic error. She realized in that brief puff of time that no good outcome can come from one whose motivation is hate. And her dead mother's mercy and love had already begun to transform the tribes in Calderont even before her intervention in the Hall of the Covenant. She could not betray those instincts, for in her mother's kindness would spin a new world with every possibility.

Her final epiphany occurred in this tick of time, for history would now pivot on what she would do. She fell in tears from Garantapede's back and lay weeping. When she finally opened her eyes, the armies of the drones were gone. Before her stood Drougen, the wise, and Salasar, the comforter. Her final test was met. She had conquered her rage. Her quest could now begin, for she had slain the dragons within before she was to confront the demons from without.

CHAPTER 11:
REVELATION

Chrysallia's journey to discovery would not be complete until she learned the meaning of her dream. She was discomforted that an inner energy could actually transmit events in her life before they occurred. Beyond that, what was the motive of this force to send such messages? Elements of her dream appeared in all her trials; that was clear. The boy at the lake, Viladon at the tree, and the little boy in white were all manifestations rooted in a later reality. The missing piece was the old man in her reverie who was walking toward the tree she was trying to avoid. "Why was he sad? Why didn't he talk to me? Why haven't I met him yet?" Without these answers she was hesitant to go forward on her journey.

She decided to confront Drougen, who was in her mind responsible for her nightmarish flight. Facing him, she exclaimed petulantly, "I have earned the right to know the meaning of my dream. Will you let me proceed in this quest not knowing its message? My father always warned me of the dragon within. What does my dream tell me of mine?"

Before answering her question, Drougen led her and Salasar to a quiet glade at the lower reaches of the peak upon which they stood when Chrysallia almost destroyed an entire civilization. He did not want her distracted by the calamities of the world she was being sent to transform. He bade her sit on the soft grass so she would feel the earth under her and began: "My dear Princess, all dreams have many messages. The figures in them can represent many things, all of which can be equally true. And the messages are in layers, each with a deeper meaning for one who can understand."

Chrysallia looked at him inquisitively. "Does my dream have more than one meaning?"

Drougen nodded. "Yes, it does. I will tell you the one you need to know now, and I will tell you the other when you return from your quest."

Chrysallia challenged him, "Why can't I know both now?"

Knowing the impatience of the young, he responded, "Because the second meaning will not provide enlightenment until you experience the full import of your quest. To tell you now would subtract from that experience, and that I will not do."

Realizing she had little choice, Chrysallia acquiesced, and Drougen began, "As I told you, the most important aspect of your dream is that the darkness you sought to escape at the tree could not be avoided. No matter how far you distanced yourself from it, it still caught up with you when you least expected. There is a message in that. What must be faced cannot be deferred, and our inner energy will always transmit that. That is the purpose of dreams—to get you to see in sleep what you refuse to acknowledge when awake. In all the ancient writings, the sages and prophets knew that when their deities wished to communicate with them, they did so by sending a dream."

Chrysallia was enrapt and pressed him: "I have always wondered who sends the messages. Who do you think does?"

Drougen paused a good while before answering in a grave tone, "As you live your life, it may be your lot to listen in silence to the voice within. For many the voice cannot be accessed in the company of others, and so they retreat to the forests and deserts so no other voices are heard but the silent one that speaks without words. It is a voice that abides in us all. It is a force that exists in all things and the empty spaces between all things. The wise never fear death or prophecy. They accept what comes because they know that the Force of the Universe is in them whispering their truth, and their lives will conclude in the embrace of that truth. That is a stream that in time you will enter. Whoever swims there never resists the current."

Captivated, Chrysallia urged him to answer a question with which she had greatly struggled or she would not trust the energy of which he spoke: "Why does it send these messages? Is it to punish us? What is its reason?"

Without hesitation, Drougen replied, "Love."

A long silence followed as Chrysallia took her measure of Drougen's response. "What if the message is a frightening one, like mine? How can that be love?"

Drougen struggled too because he knew he would have to use analogies that would make sense to one of such tender an age. "Do you believe your father, Salasand, and your mother, Beldonia, love you?"

Without hesitation Chrysallia said, "Yes, of course I do."

Drougen continued, "Has there ever been an instance when either of them warned you of a danger you had to face?"

Chrysallia's eyes widened in acknowledgment, and she nodded her head. "My father warned me that I would suffer like him if I did not kill my dragons within before facing the ones without."

Drougen was pleased and saw his advantage. "And why did he warn you of this?"

Reliving that moment of intimacy, Chrysallia responded, "He wanted me to know the consequences of acting in anger."

Drougen, nodding in affirmation, continued. "So it is with our inner power. It knows all things, including the dragons we must face to lead an authentic life, to find our way back home to the Force from whence we came. It is beyond the reasoning of a father and mother because it knows what they cannot-the outcome of all existence, and so it sends the messages, which can be found in a thousand places, not just in dreams. And for those that miss the message, they will come back into being until they see all that was missed in their previous life journeys."

Enthralled, Chrysallia was beginning to feel a strength gestating within her as she listened to these words. If what Drougen said was true, her life would have an order and outcome already known by a Force that saw what she could not. She had one more query before Drougen would explain her dream: "What if the dreamer misses the message and suffers because of it?"

Drougen began to reassess the capacity of the child before him. Her thoughts belied her years. "My young Princess, you ask excellent questions. Most of us will miss the message until we fail and suffer. That's when the answer comes, as you have found out. Know this: our failure is not a punishment but a blessing. It is the pain that opens our eyes, that leads us to sorrow, to forgiveness, and ultimately to love as we witness in others our own shortcomings. The Energy of which I speak never punishes in the way the alien priests claim. How could a force that knows all outcomes, including the behavior of those we call evil, punish them for acting out what it knew they would do eons before they came into existence? This I do not believe, and that is why I say that the motive for its messages is love even when suffering comes of it. For humans there is no compassion without it."

Satisfied, Chrysallia was ready to learn the message of a dream that threatened to end her life. "Does the dream foretell my death?" Chrysallia queried.

The wise spirit of the forest responded, "If it did, you would not be here. Your dream does address a death, but not a physical one. Let us examine the sequence for your answer. The beheaded Viladon tells you that you must die. What were the circumstances that led you to kill him in real life?"

Chrysallia thought and responded, "He wanted to take me, so I cut off his head."

Drougen followed with a second question: "What was your emotion when you did this?"

"Hate and rage," she responded.

"And did your father not tell you that hate and rage prevent any act from being heroic?" he replied.

"Yes, he did. And he told me that because of his rage, the dragon got his revenge on him. My father did not want that to happen to me," she answered.

Drougen took a few paces, hesitated, and turned. "Viladon represents the animal instinct to attack, to solve things violently. The children represent your childhood and its purity. That is why the boys wore white, and that is why they were denied access to the realm beyond the gate where the river god and his nymph were in passionate embrace. It is the instinct to couple that separates children from adults, and these young boys were not ready for that.

"Therefore, it is clear the gate represents the barrier between childhood and maturity. You were moved to desires that were dormant in those children. You found out later that had you given in to those desires with the young man by the lake, you would have deferred your quest, and a dragon would have won. So your message is clear. Your animal instinct to react to anger must die; you must leave the security of childhood and you must control your passions, or you will be unable to achieve anything.

"Your desire to remain with the children at the Portal of Innocence is a sign that the desire to remain in childhood is strong for all the young and even some adults. It is the paradise of irresponsibility that is the perfect and necessary abode for young children but inappropriate for those old enough to begin their own journey. Your dream is an affirmation that you were ready to conquer these obstacles, and this you have done in your three trials. The immersion into water at the end of your dream means that you entered that which restrained you, conquered it, and instead of fearing the tree from whence you fled, you actually mounted it and played in the branches. Most importantly, Viladon was gone once you were reborn through the water."

"You left something out," Chrysallia reminded him. "Who was the old man that didn't speak to me? Why was he moving in the opposite direction, and why haven't I met him yet in my journey?"

Drougen smiled. "But you have."

Chrysallia searched her memory. She had encountered so many figures and events in so short a span that she thought maybe she had missed an interlude or person, but she could come up with none. She looked quizzically at Drougen. "No, I have not."

The gaunt figure before her twinkled. "And who stands before you now?"

Aghast, Chrysallia blurted, "You?"

The old man of the forest laughed out loud. "Indeed. Me. And maybe your father, even though he is still young, for the Force can use anything or anyone as a symbol. He and I are forest creatures. We entered the realm of the unexplored because it is in the uncharted places where all answers lie. Your father and I met many times when he was a mere lad. I instructed him. That is why he came back. And when I was young, it was to the badlands and wild places that

I was drawn. I was frightened to death, but I cast off all tethers and went. I have learned much for the effort. We must all move in the direction of that which is not experienced or else we will be trapped in childhood forever."

But Chrysallia was not satisfied. "Why didn't you speak to me? Why did you look sad?"

Drougen patted Salasar's head, and she purred at his touch. He then faced his princess. "What could I have told you? Even at your tender age, you have come to know that words can be useless to the untested. What if I told you why you had to face the tree? What good would it have done you? Compare the weight of my possible words to the actual initiation you experienced, and you have your answer. Now that the symbols of your fantasy have been embraced, my interpretation makes sense. Without your experience, whatever I said would just be a story."

Chrysallia was transfixed. It all made sense now. The trials were anticipated by her dream. The force within had prepared her, and her success was a message that she was ready for this undertaking. She had fulfilled the lesson of her father by facing the inner animal that pulls one away from higher cause. She hoped for a deeper relationship with this force and said as much to Drougen. "Is there more? Will the second meaning bring me closer to the stream of which you speak?"

Drougen smiled as he saw in Chrysallia the light all mentors seek in the eyes of students to whom they bring instruction. He nodded in affirmation. "Yes, it will, but you are not ready for that now. When you return from the mountain, I will tell you."

But Drougen had not finished his instruction. "There is one more task you must complete before you go forward to battle the wills of six powerful men. For this undertaking, you will need a different kind of weapon, and you must use a deception that plays to their greed and power, or they will not follow you. Come, there is something I must give you." With that, Drougen selected a limb that extended to the breath of him, and he fashioned it into a staff. Then he rose, and Chrysallia fell in behind him and the mystical Salasar as they departed the glen.

CHAPTER 12:
A FLOWER FOR CHRYSALLIA

With Drougen's revelation, Chrysallia almost felt that she was with child even though she knew that was an impossibility. Yet she felt a presence growing within that made her tremble. Her moment was at hand. Her mission grave. Her words would come, but she knew even now that she would not be the author of those words. She said nothing and followed her two guardians. Drougen spoke little as well. But when he looked at her, his eyes widened, for he noticed an aura that bespoke of one chosen by destiny to change history.

The old man of the woods led them midway down the near slope to a mountain pass that cut deep into the forest at the tree line. Like a constricting snake, it wound its way around the elevations it bisected, only to disappear at the face of a most unusual range of mesas and buttes dominated by a tapered mountain peak whose mile-long base gave it the appearance of a funnel. Its apex looked like a conduit for lightning bolts, and when Chrysallia touched any point of its façade, she felt an energy. The mesas themselves were made of luminescent stone so that there was an eerie glow about them, especially at night.

Drougen began an ascent of the peak where a slight fissure in its walls allowed a trickle of water to feed an array of ferns and laurel, while miniature conifers congregated in formations at its lowest reach. As they climbed, the fissure gradually widened, and a waft of the most seductive aromas reached them from a passage that had to extend to a place not exclusive to stone. It was here that Drougen stopped, for what lay beyond had never been seen by human eyes as no one but he, the forest guardian, knew where the crease in the rock led.

As they penetrated the stony corridor, the passage was so narrow they could feel the bony probes scraping one part of their bodies and then another. The walls were damp, and they had to squeeze with great effort through the more narrow turns, which only increased Chrysallia's anxiety.

As the light from the entrance quickly faded, the darkness closed in ominously. They had no torch, and if it weren't for Drougen's knowledge of the dark path, this would have been the point where even the most seasoned explorer would turn round and retreat. This they did not do. Drougen led, and Salasar followed with Chrysallia again using the great cat's tail as her compass. There was no end to the darkness, no opening to a wider vault, and no ability to see where this conduit led. Wind whistled through the passage, adding to the macabre eeriness of the place. They felt as if they were in a crypt. Even Salasar was emitting low panting growls in her fear, for she had never experienced so deathlike an environment.

Then something happened to Chrysallia that steeled her nerves and gave her hope. As her heartbeat soared in fright, she immediately experienced again the darkness and panic of her dream. The descent into darkness was becoming a reality once more. But now the venue was different. She was in the darkened womb of this mystical mountain, and she prayed a rebirth was awaiting her should she see the light of day if ever the mountain decided to expel them. Another death. Another metamorphosis. But to what? Would she rise again as she did in the tree?

The promise of that possibility was the subtle, enticing bouquets of scent coming from some point or place beyond these encroaching crevices. Except for the scraping sound of her feet and Drougen's staff probing the walls, smell was the only beacon they had, and it was emanating from somewhere decidedly closer, because the aromas were becoming more pronounced. Time could not be gauged without visible movement or light, but in what seemed a small eternity, faint illuminations began to reveal the texture of the walls and floor of the mountain's innards. The passage widened, and their pace quickened. Then there was light. Light, the hope that lies when the unseen becomes visible. Light, the end of chaos and the harbinger of order. Light, the forerunner of the Word.

In the span of a few heartbeats the cavern yawned an opening, and they were released from its dark grip. What lay before them had never been framed by human eyes, for they were witnessing what seemed like the final act of creation before bipeds began their era of predation. A vast crater rich in soil and fertilized by myriads of birds that made the crannies and niches of the elevation their home opened to an enclosed plain below. There the grazing beasts feasted on the nutrient grasses, and their numbers were kept in balance by feline and canine predators anointed to keep this harmony undisturbed and eternal.

But it was the sides to the chasm that caught the eye. Two narrow waterfalls poured down the far façade facing them equidistant from each other. Whether through time or cosmic disturbance, the vaults between them were terraced as if carved by some unseen hand intent on providing sanctuary to a profusion of pastel-colored flowers and vines. And ledges at every level extended out like the decorous flowerboxes of some appointed deity to catch the gentle mist and spray of the descending water. Each flow was interrupted by rock formations encasing pools of crystal liquid before allowing the pour to continue its unhurried journey downward.

It was as if some mystical rainbow was momentarily transformed into a prism that shattered into the floral arrangements nestled in the bedrock. Adding to the rapturous display were blue and yellow hummingbirds feverishly drinking the nectar proffered by the generous stamens and sepals of the floral inhabitants of the terraces. And songbirds of every hue and shade trilled their contentment as they cavorted in the pools and feasted on the never ending bounty of seed released by the regenerating blooms. But seed was not their exclusive offering. Each had its own subtle scent that induced an ecstasy even in the beasts. Salasar herself was caught in this ritual as she rolled on her back in the throes of contentment.

At the center of this edenic panorama was a single white flower to whom the rest traced their origin and to whom they paid special obeisance. Larger than the rest, emanating its own aura, ensconced in a preeminent altar of loam and stone, it stood unique. Chrysallia was enthralled at its beauty and dominance. Even from where she stood, she could see its center was flecked with what looked like a splash of every other species' tint and shade, the significance of which would be impressed upon her with closer examination. She also espied its cuplike core that collected the ionized water from the pristine droplets rebounding all around it.

Drougen pointed profoundly. "This is why you are here."

Chrysallia raised her eyebrows in wonderment. "For this flower? It is truly the most beautiful I have ever seen, even more comely than the sarquellas, which are my favorite. But what am I to do with it?"

Drougen paused and then looked deep into her eyes. "Change the world."

Still staring at the flower in wonderment, Chrysallia received the revelations of Drougen. He told her the flower was indestructible, that it represented the ever-regenerating earth from which no physical thing could ever truly be destroyed. It was said that if its petals were consumed and its liquid drunk, the seeker would be transformed to new illumination. Death would lose its sting and the awareness that the only real changes are changes in form would be realized. A new consciousness that the Energy remains present in all things would follow and a reverence for these things would begin because of it. Violence would end.

"This is what you must deliver to the kingdoms of contention threatening our world. Words or threats will have no effect on them, and if you were to use weapons such as the hordes of Garantapede, you become the thing you wish to replace, as both your mother and father knew. The mystery of this flower will bring them to the vision needed to reverse their dark slide to cataclysm and destruction. Go and remove it from its encasement. Your final journey now begins."

With that, Chrysallia followed the narrow pathway circumventing the crater's rim to where the flower reigned. At this, Salasar knew her function as guide was over and descended to the crater floor to feast on the herds feeding there. Like the flower at the summit, she would reign supreme on the plain below.

Chrysallia had to keep her eyes firmly riveted on the narrow walkway upon which she trod. The vista before her was so alluring and so captivating that its sensory delights almost caused her to lose footing. Again she realized how easy it was to become distracted and lose your way even to the noblest of ends. She did not look up again. The path descended before the Flower of Life, and she had to approach it from below.

The ledges formed a natural stairway so that upon reaching the final step, Chrysallia was face to face with a force of beauty more powerful than any weapon or artifact crafted in the forges of men. It radiated light, silence, redolence, regeneration, and unity. For there at the base of each petal were flecks of color that reflected the hue and stain of every other flower in the crater. Here were the many joined in the one in a harmony that bespoke the nature of her mission with the kingdoms of intolerance awaiting her. She prayed her words could capture that which was so eloquently revealed in the petals of a single flower. If only men could see, she thought. Eternity is here. The evidence is at hand.

Chrysallia reverentially lifted the flower from its encasement and compulsively brought it to her waiting lips. She lifted it in sacred ritual and, with eyes closed, drank the liquid accumulated from the droplets of ageless streams whose journeys mirrored the same eternity as that of the petals.

As the draft coursed through her, a sensation began to emanate from her own spiritual wellspring. Unlike the icy dragon's blood that robbed her father of vitality, this nectar generated a warmth and clarity that enabled her to feel connected to all life and to that which lies in the spaces enveloping all life. She was part of a design, and the love she felt for the source and all its manifestations brought tears to her eyes. How could such a gift be bestowed on one so callow as her, she reflected, a young girl about to descend to a world where young girls were not invited to higher callings nor perceived of as anything but frivolous. She knew her journey would shatter these and other mind-sets. Turning, she retraced her steps back to the waiting Drougen.

The old man struggled to keep his composure as he witnessed the event that would reshape his universe. His words were heavy with emotion as he welcomed her to the cavern entrance again. "Your time is at hand, Princess. Of all who walk, wade, or fly, you have been chosen to restore the land and the sky above it. My work is almost done. When we reach the threshold of the clan kingdoms, I will give you final instruction on what you must do. Then you must proceed alone, and I must return to my abode in the remote woods."

Chrysallia, even though reassured by the power of this sacred flower, looked anxiously for her guardian cat, her totem, the mysterious Salasar. She did not want to go forth alone into the kingdoms of conflict without her. It was as if this feline of contradictions was the very ground of her own being, her light in the uncharted forests, her comfort in the last conscious moment before sleep, and the seat of all her passion and exuberance. She no more wanted to proceed without Salasar now than she would have wanted to go to bed as a child without her stuffed panther at her pillow. She could not sleep without it, and even though her dependency on this bedside companion had waned as she grew older, it never left her chambers.

Searching the plain below for any sign of her, Chrysallia, almost childlike again, turned to Drougen. "Where is my cat? I need her. She is my protector and my companion. I love her."

The old man of the forest had anticipated this moment, and as her tutor, he would have to prepare her for the crucible to come. "Princess, Salasar has fulfilled her function. Soon I will fulfill mine and leave you. In your dream, the eight little boys wanted to go with you beyond the gate. It was not their time to do so, for what you were about to learn had to be experienced alone. There comes a time in all our journeys when instruction and support must end. Our truth must then be discovered without the benefit of companionship, for it is in the casting off that you find your true self. It is witnessed at birth, and it is witnessed at death. The infant's cord to the mother must be cut. In that moment it is physically separated from its source. In time there are other cords and other chains unseen that must also be cut. Any departure from the familiar is a cutting of a cord, and it is only through these departures that your inner possibilities are activated. They will never come to light if you live a life of comfort.

"When you saw the old man in your dream walking toward the tree and the darkness, he was alone. He was sad when he saw you as I am sad now knowing that you and all youth will have to take the same path into the unknown unaccompanied. You will never know your full measure or that of your fellow travelers if this does not happen. And when the final departure arrives, the cord to your physical life will be cut so you may be born again forever and that will be the end of all separation as you return in the embrace of the One."

Chrysallia knew Drougen was right, yet she felt compelled to ask a final question: "Will I see her again?"

"Yes," Drougen replied, "when you return from your quest; you must re-place the Flower. Then you will see Salasar once more, the purpose of which I cannot reveal now."

Even with that Chrysallia still felt deserted. What Drougen didn't tell her was the anguish of a good-bye when a door is closed at a journey's end. She took her last look, and with the Flower of Life in her hand, she preceded Drougen into the darkness again.

CHAPTER 13:
A PLAN OF PERSUASION

The return through the dark corridor was different from their initial foray. The Flower provided illumination, and with Chrysallia leading, the passage was less precarious. Yet the space was still cramped and uncomfortable, and she yearned for release from the pressing stone. It came to her that in this funnel from darkness to light, she was being born again. A part of her was incubating on the way through and a part of her was emerging on the way out. Something precious was left behind, and something precious was going with her. Her life kept pivoting on what seemed a never ending cycle of regeneration. Looking back at her first incursion into Fendor and taking measure of herself now at its farthest reach, she had gone through so much. Her inner voice spoke in symbols of the import of her journey, and her physical initiations in the forest confirmed the message. Now the reason for her mission was taking its final form.

Drougen took her to the point where Garantapede and his lethal horde were set to descend on the unsuspecting federations below and obliterate them. From this platform Chrysallia scanned a panorama of great bustle and activity. The inhabitants of the six kingdoms below appeared to her like automatons mindlessly going about the daily regimens of buying and selling, exploiting and consuming, fighting and dying—totally oblivious to the consequences of the drama they were acting out. Despite wars and natural disasters, their numbers swelled to such a degree that they lived in an ever-shrinking world that could not provide resources consistent with their numbers. And the more removed they became from their remaining forest precincts and wet-lands, the more violently they behaved.

She could also see and hear the sounds of worship from impressive edifices of glass and stone. But the devotion of the worshipers was rooted in a belief that they were chosen to hold sway over all others. The problem was that six kingdoms held to this same tenet, so there was no end to persecution, attempts at conversions, violent or otherwise, and an abiding intolerance that made for a precarious existence. And in the midst of all manner of wealth for the few, the pious were oblivious to the squalor and disease of those unable to rise to material opportunity.

Drougen also surveyed the expanse as he had done many times before when he fretfully observed the flight of thousands seeking refuge from their theaters of conflict into the deserts of Zod and the forest of Fendor. He couldn't help but take pity on them despite the threat they represented, for he knew they were seeking sanctuary. In exchange for sustenance, they would reveal to him the history and mores of their places of origin. In this manner he gained insight into the machinations of the rulers of each realm. This information proved invaluable to Chrysallia's mission, because armed with this intelligence, she could exploit them to her end.

Drougen directed her eyes eastward and began to identify each of the six domains as they stretched from the outer fringes of Fendor to the encroaching deserts of Zod in the west. He pointed to his far right and spoke. "The first kingdom to the east is the land of the Terruleans. Their leader is called Targon. He is very warlike but equally clever. Targon will use force or guile depending on his advantage. Be wary of his temper. Be equally wary of his impulses toward you. He is used to getting his way with women.

"Next is the land of the Shui. Their ruler is called Dai. He is a master at being underestimated and as a result has grown in power and influence under the nose of his adversaries. His people fear foreigners as does he. Dai will feign humility to gain your trust while he entertains you. His guests will be spies seeking to uncover your mission. Make them believe you can enrich them over their neighbors, and they will encourage Dai to do your bidding.

"At the northern extreme above the land of the Shui is Liguria. Their leader is called Caravinus. He is drawn to beauty on the one hand and power on the other. When his passions are enflamed, he can be more violent even than Targon. He will be distracted by your youth and comely appearance. In this he is vulnerable.

"To the south of the Shui is the land of the Compalla. Their chieftain is Mboya. He is a man struggling between the old and the new. While he is in competition with the other federations, much of his efforts are invested in uniting his own tribes. He will be open to you if you can convince him there is gain for his people."

Drougen then shifted her scan to the far western expanse to the left bordering on the desert of Zod. "The people of the Riff are led by the chieftain Kazak. He is a severe man who follows the ways of the tribes in all his dealings. He is rigid in this but generous in his acceptance of the stranger as a guest. He will struggle with your gender. Be indirect when speaking to him. His conflict with the other kingdoms consumes him. If he senses you can help him in this, it will override his other considerations.

"Last we come to the tribes of the Yesh people. Their confederation is governed by Dovin, who, like his counterpart Kazak, follows the codes he inherited from the ancient times in all he does. You will see an instant similarity between him and Kazak, for their beliefs and looks are almost identical. Yet they have been enemies since they can remember. They have influenced the other kingdoms with their sacred writings, but all take what covenants suit them and to their own purpose.

"Underlying the disparities between them is a destructive sense of superiority that is not just rooted in their beliefs. You will see that each of them presents different features and shades of color to the skin, which have been imprinted in each culture as the yardstick for what constitutes beauty. Any deviation from that image is regarded as less than desirable, and so even their physical appearances are a source of contention between them. And their priests use this as a means of keeping them separate. For some, any comingling would carry the weight of exile."

Chrysallia saw before her in cosmic proportion what she faced with the remnants of these dark credos in the Hall of the Covenant before she left Calderont. It was amazing to her that the people of this universe could live in such conflict and fear since their origins and not do anything to reverse it.

Drougen, the all wise, would enlighten her in this even further. "My dear Princess," he exclaimed, "these kingdoms have been involved in wars without end for millennia. They have scarcely escaped but a few years' peace and then jump into the firestorm again. This is what you must reverse, because the illness from which they suffer comes from the eyes. When they first open in the morning, their enemies are staring back at them. And the possibilities that exist from what they cannot see do not haunt their dreams at night. That message and that enlightenment must now come from you. This is why you have been called-to make them see possibility in what they have yet to conceive. If you are successful, their universe will crash and a new era of promise will ensue that will change our realm in the forests as well. Our trees and streams will hold to their purity, and the Spirit Force will be seen in all things because of the new vision you will provide."

Chrysallia, ever evolved from crossing the thresholds that transformed her, could not grasp why she, instead of her father or the sage Pentamon, was chosen for this cosmic challenge. She needed to know this to steel her will to the task. Confronting Drougen, she pressed him for an answer. "Why have I, a young girl, been called to undertake a quest that an army would struggle to achieve?"

Drougen nodded knowingly. "Because the pendulum of time must swing to the center once again. This last cycle for them has been defined by the rule of men. Even their deity is a man. And the things of men not softened by the heart have held sway for much of their existence. To challenge them with violence just makes them harder. They have become inured to systems fueled by power, dominance, violence, and mindless consumption. All their science serves these ends. Not one of these before you is capable of compassion for his brother. They all fear the heart and extol an emotionless logic in its stead.

"This is why their females have been for the most part excluded from rule lest they become sensitive or weak. Men rule through iron and steel, women from the heart. No, Princess, it is not from an army of men that they will find redemption, but from the mystique and compassionate power of the woman. And the Spirit Force from our world has chosen you as that woman. Sit and I will reveal what I have been instructed to give you."

With this Chrysallia, chosen among women to redeem what no man could, humbly took a place upon the rarefied ground of Fendor before confronting the next crucible awaiting her in the physical and parochial world of men. She would now receive her final instruction and then go forward to face kings and chieftains armed with only a flower.

But before he spoke, Drougen led her to a cache nestled in a rocky compartment where a better view of the deserts of Zod could be obtained. Removing the boulder from whence it was encased, Drougen extracted a tote and revealed its contents to Chrysallia. She was startled at what she saw. "What is this? It looks like wax, and what are these six sashes and a cord for?"

The old man took one of the folds out and tied it around Chrysallia's eyes. Startled, she quickly removed it only to see Drougen smile knowingly. "There is a purpose to this, as you shall see. We will prepare your way into the kingdoms by summoning the pigeons of good King Althius. They will act as our messengers much in the same way as they were used to call forth your father to slay the Dragon of Maladour. They will whisper in the ears of the kings and people that you are a prophetess from Calderont who knows of a treasure that, once obtained, will ensure the dominance of one of the kingdoms above all others. Of course, each will assume that they will be the beneficiary of this bounty and follow you to its source. You will convince them that all six must accompany you and that they should bring with them the sacred text to which they all defer. Here is where you will take them."

With this, Drougen positioned her so that she could see a massive and extraordinary elevation at the far north of Zod. "This is Asperion, the sacred mountain at the end of their universe. It is the source of Revelation and Transformation. When the Spirit Force wishes to speak, this is the place between the heavens and earth where the message becomes Word. You are to lead them to its base. There will be six paths leading to the top. You will order them to fast for seven days and to contemplate their holy books before ascending. Tell them the one who arises to the pinnacle will receive the treasure and rule their world. The others will kneel in subordination and all things will be transformed. This will occur when the anointed one opens the sacred chest embedded for centuries in the undisturbed stone. What will occur then will be revealed to you as you see it with your kings for the first time."

Chrysallia, transfixed at this message, queried, "But how will I get to the top?"

The old man pointed to two giant forms hovering in the sky above them. "On the wings of eagles."

The princess trembled, for it was clear that she, like her father before her, was destined to act out a drama that would alter the direction of the physical and spiritual world.

"And to what purpose are the wax and the sashes?" she asked.

Drougen's eyes narrowed. "When you enter Zod, the priests invested in separation will unleash an army of demons to prevent this journey, for they know they will be cast out if your quest is realized. These energies are very powerful and very dangerous. They have each held their respective kingdoms in their grip from the beginning, and they will not release them lightly. You will see what seems a great storm of dust and darkness. Immediately stuff the ears of the kings with the wax and blindfold them with the sashes. Bind them each to the tether and lead them until the demons relent at the futility of impeding you. Hold the Flower of Life in front of you, for they will have no power over it."

With that, Drougen took a giant pole leaning against the rock where the tote was entombed. He began to wave it in a circular motion for several minutes. Of a sudden the sky was full with the pigeons of King Althius. They swooped to the realms below to complete their assigned task. Drougen then handed the tote to the Princess of Possibility and spoke in a cautionary tone: "Keep the Flower in the tote, for it must not be used indiscriminately or its energy will diminish. You must return it to its appointed place when your mission is completed. Then I will guide you back to Calderont."

Chrysallia's time had come.

CHAPTER 14:
INTO THE MAELSTROM

For the first time since she entered Fendor, Chrysallia was all alone. Clutching her tote, she descended into a world she did not know to become the sole instrument that could redeem it. She did as Drougen had commanded, visiting each kingdom beginning with the Terruleans. Hearing of her coming by the messenger pigeons of King Althius, Chrysallia was accorded every honor. Banquets were held and gifts bestowed as if she were some prophetess of promise. Targon and his peers all reacted to her as Drougen had predicted, and for some with dire consequences. While she was with the Terruleans, one of Targon's minions aspired to learn the contents of her tote with the hope of gaining access to the secret treasure. When he opened it, he tried to remove the contents and was blinded by the flower. While in the hands of the pure, it was the essence of life. To a defiler, it was the opposite.

Chrysallia was more than aware of the transgression, as was her mystical capacity when she slew Viladon and feigned outrage to Targon. She used the incident to her advantage and told him he risked elimination from the quest should any further transgressions occur. Targon, who had less than honorable intentions with her, was immediately pliant in her company. He knew his enemies would celebrate his exclusion, and he warned all in his court that any further disrespect to Chrysallia would be met by torture and death. With this advantage, Chrysallia deftly implied the treasure would be his in return for his fealty. For Targon, greed was a stronger appetite than his lust for Chrysallia. He submitted to her.

The news of the incident with the flower traveled far and wide, and no further violations occurred. Caravinus, however, was so taken with her beauty that he plied her with music, feasts, and jewelry to gain favor. Unlike Targon, wealth was a secondary consideration for him. Knowing his pride and unbounded ardor, she struck at his sense of manhood to cool him. Recounting her dream and her experience with her own lust at the lake, the young princess revealed to the passionate Caravinus that men subordinate to their appetites were unfit for heroic callings and that perhaps he should anoint one from his ranks who had greater self-control. Infuriated but aware of this truth, he desisted and saw in this young girl a wisdom that belied her tender years. A profound respect for her followed. She knew his tragic flaw and blunted it as no other could.

She left a similar impression on Dai. As he diplomatically probed her experiences with the other kings, Dai was hoping for intelligence that he could use to his advantage. He was a master strategist, and as Drougen had foretold, spies were assigned to follow her in hopes of ascertaining her plans and intentions. As they sat cross-legged at a state dinner, Chrysallia whispered to him her awareness of all his machinations and pointed out his spies to him. He was outmaneuvered by a child and lost face to one of greater political acumen than he who was regarded as the master. Seeing the futility of any further deception, he too acquiesced to her.

Her encounter with Mboya was equally effective. Her simplicity in her dealings with him and her advice on his one issue of paramount importance—the unification of his own people—won him over. Till now, Mboya had relied on suppression to achieve his ends. Recounting her own experience with the tribes in Calderont, Chrysallia related how the creation of a Council for Unity brought the contending clans together. She demonstrated how the invitation to empowerment resulted in the desired unification not the application of violence. Mboya had his answer, and he saw in her wisdom beyond that of his closest advisors, and from that point he trusted her.

She was no less impressive with Kazak and Dovin. Realizing their strict prescription of accepted roles and dress for men and women, Chrysallia donned the proper shawl and veil of each culture and behaved accordingly.

She was indirect when she had to be and forceful when called for. From what she learned from Pentamon regarding their histories, she was able to quote the deeds of women revered by them both and so was accepted as if she were one of them. The difference was the gift she was bearing, which both Kazak and Dovin greatly coveted. In this they were forced to defer to her.

In her private moments with each chieftain, Chrysallia told her tale as one sent to enrich his kingdom, and each was captivated by the possibility of gaining the treasure that would at last ensure his stewardship over his universe. The lust for power superseded any suspicion, for Chrysallia commanded that they follow her instructions to the smallest detail, or she would withdraw.

Within a week's time the six were to assemble at the southern tip of Zod and prepare for a forty-day journey into the desert. They would include in their possessions their sacred texts, which, when contemplated, would ensure the ascent of one of them to the peak of Asperion and the treasure. The rest would then be subordinate to the victor, and therein would begin the new order. Each was convinced by Chrysallia that he was the chosen one and that the others had to participate in the journey to witness the triumph and then kneel in submission to the new master. The anticipation of such power was intoxicating, but the outcome would be far beyond anything any of them contemplated.

Their goal was to arrive at the foothills of Mount Asperion, the sacred mountain known to their ancestors as the place of Revelation. Their rivalry would cease during their time in the desert as a consequence of Chrysallia's mission. When they reached the floor of the mount, Chrysallia would assign them a path, and after a week's fast and contemplation of their sacred texts, the climb would begin.

At the appointed time the men arrived at the desert's edge. Provisions were provided them by nomadic tribesmen who lived on the semiarid fringes of Zod. These people were friendly since they were without affiliation except to the desert. The austerity of the climate and the need to wander from oasis to oasis to avoid overconsumption made for a simple life without the need for ambition. There was also a spiritual cast to them that was contagious. It was as if the lack of material distraction invited them to a deeper awareness of natural forces rather than the false bustle of commerce and advancement.

Their serenity was compelling. It made the men sense what was missing in their own lives.

Dressed in the garb of the nomads, it was difficult to estimate their status, for they no longer looked like kings or chieftains. The effect was not lost on them either. This leveling of station to that of pilgrims on a journey generated a hint of camaraderie reminiscent of men going off on a hunt or a jaunt in the forest as an escape from the world of merchants and money lenders.

As the days passed, their sense of adventure gave way to monotony. The routine of traversing the dunes, resting during the heat of the day, and eating around evening campfires invited diversion.

Chrysallia had anticipated all this and was unusually silent with them. Coming from a place unknown and being a young girl, there was to their mind little to talk about with her. They shared nothing in common, so the men, as was their wont, engaged each other. They began to regale themselves with tales of adventure and bawdy stories with women when they thought Chrysallia was out of range and humorous anecdotes that each favored when entertaining at traditional fetes. Raucous laughter punctuated the silence of the desert. A change was subtly intruding on their age-long resentments. They were becoming more human, and of greater consequence, they were becoming aware of each other's humanity, especially at night. The longing for home, the absence of their children, and the support of their wives were common topics of conversation. This softened them.

But from the inner sanctums of the priestly temples in each of the kingdoms such empathy could prove disastrous. The dark spirits that fed on division and exclusion were not unaware of the bonding in the desert threatening walls of separation that had taken centuries to cultivate. The land began to tremble as each demonic force emerged from its underground habitation to undo what this young girl was generating in the wasteland. In increasing fury they converged, and in the form of a dark windstorm they coursed across the desert toward the men they had invested in to maintain their grip in a divided world.

Chrysallia saw the whirlwind on the horizon coming toward them at great speed. The men thought it was a typical sandstorm not uncommon in the land of Zod. Opening her tote she immediately bound them to her tether so they would not lose each other to the swirling dust. She also made them stop their ears with beeswax and cover their eyes with the sashes so these senses could be protected from the raging wind. This they did just as the demons were upon them. Chrysallia was fortunate to unleash the Flower of Life as the whirlwind of rage and venom descended. Had she not provided them with this protection, the quest would have ended there in the remote desert.

In a great circular motion each demon picked his man and howled every vile curse in his ear. The wails, almost in unison, were bloodcurdling: "Kill her. Kill the infidel. Hate preserves you. Conquer. Be merciless. It is in the Book….It is in the Book. I am the Truth, the Preserver of Your Beliefs, the Keeper of Your Temples. Strike now. Strike now…"

But the howling fell on deaf ears and the men couldn't see. They were being led to a higher place by a girl with a flower who held them together by a rope.

Through the howling maelstrom they marched, pace undiminished, as the flood of venom sought entry into their souls through their ears. But the only one who could hear them was Chrysallia, and she might as well have been deaf. The winds lost intensity, and the dark energies of division slunk back in defeat to the basements of the priestly places from whence they came.

Restored to daylight, the men removed the sashes from their eyes and the beeswax from their ears. Chrysallia loosened the ties on the tether, and there, as they shook the sand and debris from their garments, loomed Asperion, the mount that held for each of them the promise of a lifetime.

CHAPTER 15:
ASCENSION

Exhausted from their journey, they dug a pit lined with stone, made a fire, and ate their last meal together before the seven-day fast required of them would begin on the morrow. As the flames flickered across their faces in the night sky, each became lost in thought. For the first time doubt was intruding upon their beliefs. The hatred and fear so long cultivated toward their assumed foes were almost gone. Each felt a twinge at the need to dominate his brother. "Maybe there is another way? Maybe the treasure could be shared? No. Impossible. What am I thinking? It is my rightful claim. I will be generous, though, in victory." And so their sleep was haunted by these wavering possibilities.

Dawn announced her presence with a ribbon of pink and golden splash skirting the night sky at the horizon. In the pristine desert air the last embers of the evening fire were losing life, and slowly each man was restored to the world of shapes and structure. Before them stood Chrysallia. Their trial was at hand. Heartbeats raised in anxiety, the men awaited their instruction.

Chrysallia told them to remove their sacred texts from their bindle sacks. "How many of you have read these works in their entirety undisturbed by another's interpretation?" she inquired. The men grew uneasy, for none of them had. Each was given instruction on the meaning and importance of each passage. "Now you will discover for yourself and by yourself that which is profound to you and that which is history, for it is in the profound that you will find your answer and your ascension."

Chrysallia then separated them. Each was directed to a path leading to the top of the mountain. The distance between them was such that one could not see the others' paths. In fact, there was no way of knowing if another path even existed. All were told the same thing by the Princess of Possibility: "You are to fast for seven days. During that time, you are to read and contemplate your sacred works. On the morning of the eighth day, begin your ascent in the knowledge that the light and truth you have discovered will bring you alone to the top. There I will await you. In a casement of antiquity is a great chest wherein lies the wealth of the world. It will be yours."

With that each king cracked the first page of the holy book that was to be his catapult to the hidden riches of Asperion. All seemed to discover the poetry and clarity of their ancient texts for the first time. Some of what they read was disturbing. There was violence and seeming contradiction between the need to judge and the need to forgive. But there were other passages of pure enlightenment that transported them from historical perspective to the mystical fire that lay beyond the masks and forms of this world. The poverty of words palled at the contemplation of that which defied all vocabulary. And in the night sky as they took their rest, the vast cosmos before them confirmed that the eye and the ear could not fathom what the word tried to portray. Maybe there was meaning beyond the word. Maybe the word was the invitation to discover what lies beyond letters and symbols. None could escape the sky when lost in meditation, for that was what was before them. That and the book. Each to its purpose.

As the days passed and the fast continued, they were given to hallucination, for the food they were digesting did not go to the stomach. It went to the soul. And the soul was penetrating the physical to embrace energies not limited to the personality. The mystical was unfolding. Each of them began to experience connection to space and time. Each was distinct and yet part of a whole. The enlightenment humbled them. They wept, for the blinders of their parochial existences were being replaced by an ever-extending awareness of a Presence they were just now beginning to engage.

On the morning of the eighth day, each man began his ascent hungry, but for a lot more than treasure. Chrysallia was waiting. The two eagles had long since deposited her at Asperion's crest, and now she awaited the same discoveries that were to be revealed to the kings.

Their ascent was arduous. Each was spent from lack of food, but their passion drove them, for they were no longer men who ruled just a material kingdom. And as each began the departure from the land below, new revelations became manifest. The first was a growing sense of humility. Convinced that his inheritance from the book represented the intention of his God to bring him alone to treasure was inspiring. To be chosen by Him whose realm extended beyond all senses fueled a confidence that long would have waned without the sustenance of food.

And another thought infected them that was equally powerful. As each paused to look down on the world from which he departed, he saw the land fractured by greed and imposition. The people were lost as they, the men who ruled them, were lost until this point.

"If I am chosen to receive such gifts as to change all this, I will share this path and the beneficence it brings with my brother. It is not his fault that the Word in his book is in error. Once the light is seen, conflict will end, for the Truth will have been revealed." This they all mused as their fingers bled and their nails cracked on the unforgiving stone, challenging their will to rise.

Within three days the first king reached the pinnacle alone, or so he thought. Exhausted, he looked over all that he was ordained to rule, and it was good.

As he turned to find Chrysallia and the casement containing the power he was to inherit, there stood his brothers facing him. Each froze, for this was impossible. Something was terribly wrong. Their astonishment was mixed with confusion. "If I am the chosen one, how could this be? Did not this child inform me that I alone would ascend to this place and that the Word given to my people was the ladder to my preeminence?" This Targon, Dovin, Kazak, Caravinus, Dai, and Mboya had to confront. What did this mean?

None were prepared for the answer that was staring them in the face. **THEY WERE ALL CHOSEN.** The Word was finally revealed. "Love God. Love your neighbor" was the common inheritance of them all. For the first time, each experienced the power of the commandment. The simplest of statements had brought each to this place. No path was cursed, and no path was singularly blessed. And in that moment their universe was changed forever, for it marked the end of a religious existence and the beginning of a spiritual one.

The wise Drougen and the once mighty Salasand were right. The world does pivot on what men see when they open their eyes. For the first time in their history, six men saw the same light that guided him also flickering in his brother. How then could he pick up a weapon and strike a man or his family knowing this?

The men wept. A different inheritance than what they anticipated was awaiting them. Spent emotionally and physically, they came to Chrysallia, who was perched on a ledge above a partially hidden encasement where the treasure lay awaiting their will. Before opening it, the men speculated on what they would do with this bounty. Plans for projects, feasts, support for the poor, and reclamation of land were all discussed with relish. They would share this gift, for this was why they had all been guided by the same Word to reach this place. The time had come.

The kings and chieftains who were now just men joined to lift the formidable lid from the cavernous and ancient chest that seemed wedded to the rock embracing it. The wealth of the earth awaited them; the material means to change their world was now within the grasp of six wise men who would justly administer it.

But that was not meant to be. For when the lid was removed with consummate effort, nothing was in the casement. The men and Chrysallia herself for that matter were stunned. The chest was without gold, gem, or coin. They stood facing each other aghast. They had come so far, suffered so much, dreamt of all possibility only to peer into an empty vault. If there was treasure here, the eye could not see it.

Of a sudden a rumbling within the mountain knocked them off their feet. It was as if the opening they had forced had unleashed some titanic energy awaiting release after centuries of silence. The roar, more violent than thunder, seemed to turn stone into liquid, for the ground beneath them felt alive. They immediately felt nausea from the undulating platform beneath them. And then the blinding light compelled each man to cower face down on the ground. They thought for sure they would die at the hands of some avenging demon disturbed by their transgression. A searing heat licked at their faces and feet. Above the ledge holding the empty repository, piercing rays of light were burning through the obdurate stone. The air was filled with the odor of brimstone as the splash of incinerated slag cascaded over the crest-like demonic fireflies.

While each man trembled uncontrollably on his knees, Chrysallia was lifted off her feet and suspended in midair, her face of a glow not of this world. Then silence. The ground was solid again, the thunder dissipated, but the odor of burnt stone remained. Courage was restored to them, and they looked up.

What they saw lifted their hair as if the space enveloping them were galvanized. For above the suspended princess hovering like an angel were ten tablets inscribed by an unseen hand. If there was a treasure, it had come in a form yet to be discovered. One thing was clear. On this mountain the mortal plane was cracked by the hand of eternity.

Chrysallia looked down on them. She was covered in a soft light, her eyes filled with compassion knowing she was the instrument for a new covenant among men. When she spoke, it was not her voice:

"I HAVE CHOSEN THIS CHILD TO DELIVER MY MESSAGE UNTO YOU, WHICH YOU HAVE EARNED FROM YOUR ASCENT. REVELATION COMES AT MY CHOOSING WHEN THE TIME FOR CHANGE IS AT HAND. A NEW CYCLE MUST NOW BEGIN, FOR TO CONTINUE ON YOUR CURRENT PATH WILL LEAD TO YOUR UTTER DESTRUCTION. THAT IS NOT YOUR DESTINY. I HAVE NOT CREATED THIS WORLD TO DESTROY IT, AND I ALREADY KNOW WHAT YOU WILL DO WITH THESE WORDS AS I KNOW ALL THINGS OUTSIDE OF TIME. THERE WILL BE MORE GIVEN TO YOU WHEN THE FRUITS OF THESE BEATITUDES ARE PRACTICED. NEW CONSCIOUSNESS WILL BRING YOU CLOSER TO ALL THINGS SEEN AND UNSEEN. FOR THERE ARE GREATER MYSTERIES TO BE REVEALED WHEN YOU ARE READY. AND I KNOW WHEN THAT WILL BE.

"THE FIRST REVELATION IS ABOUT THE WORD. TO SPEAK TO YOU REQUIRES THAT I USE LANGUAGE. WHERE I AM THERE IS NO WORD. YOU CANNOT FATHOM ME WITH YOUR LETTERS AND MASKS. I AM BEYOND THEM. WORDS PREVENT THE RAPTURE BECAUSE THEY ARE CONFINED TO MEANING WITHIN YOU. YOUR UNDERSTANDING IS NOT MY UNDERSTANDING. KNOW THIS NOW. WORDS WILL LIMIT MY TRUTH. THEY INVITE INTERPRETATION, AND THEY WILL BE BENT AND SHAPED TO MEET THE NEEDS OF THOSE WHO MUST CONTROL YOU. I HAVE ALLOWED THAT, FOR WHEN THE WORD LEADS YOU TO COMMIT VIOLENCE AND IMPOSE SUFFERING, YOU WILL DOUBT IT, AND THAT IS GOOD. IT WILL BRING YOU BACK TO ME. IT IS THE WAY. YOU ARE A CREATURE THAT CANNOT LEARN WITHOUT SUFFERING AND TRANSGRESSION. IT IS HOW I BRING YOU TO LIGHT.

"I CREATED BECAUSE MY PERFECTION PREVENTS ME FROM EXPERIENCING WHAT I AM NOT. AND THAT IS YOU. THAT IS WHY YOU WERE GIVEN FORM SO THAT I CAN EXPERIENCE YOU AND MYSELF THROUGH YOU. AND I HAVE SHAPED YOU IN WAYS THAT WILL BRING YOU BACK TO ME IN GLORY. BUT IT IS THROUGH THE PATH OF CONTRADICTIONS THAT YOUR AWARENESS OF ME WILL BE OBTAINED. A MAN WILL APPRECIATE HIS FOOD WHEN HIS PLATE IS STOLEN. SO IT WILL BE WITH YOU AS YOU FATHOM THE WORLD OF GOOD AND EVIL, PLEASURE AND PAIN, LIFE AND DEATH. THOSE I HAVE ANOINTED HAVE DONE JUST THAT AND LEFT THEIR LEGACY IN YOUR BOOKS.

"I WILL GIVE YOU A VISION TO HELP YOU UNDERSTAND. IMAGINE YOU WENT TO THE OCEAN AND DIPPED A CUP INTO THE SEA. THE CUP WOULD HAVE THE SAME WATER AS THE WAVES COURSING TO THE SHORE. IT IS THE SEA IN A CUP. THE CUP IS YOU. I AM IN YOU CONFINED TO YOUR BODY. I AM ALSO THE SEA. AS YOU EXPLORE AND EXPAND TO WIDER DEPTHS AND FARTHER

SHORES, THE CUP GETS LARGER AND MORE WATER IS HELD. YOU ARE EMBRACING MORE OF THE SEA. EVENTUALLY THERE WILL BE NO MORE CUP. YOU WILL HAVE ABSORBED EVERY ISLAND AND SHORELINE UNTIL YOU AND THE SEA ARE ONE. THAT IS YOUR DESTINY. AT JOURNEY'S END YOU AND I ARE ONE.

"I ALSO EXIST BEYOND WHAT YOU CALL ETHICS. I KNOW WHAT EVERY HUMAN YOU HAVE CALLED EVIL WILL DO, AND I KNEW IT EONS BEFORE THEY WERE BORN. I CREATED THEM, FOR NOTHING IN EXISTENCE IS WITHOUT MY KNOWLEDGE OR OUTSIDE OF MY PURPOSE. I DO NOT CREATE A MAN OR A WOMAN AND THEN BECOME SURPRISED WHEN THEY CAUSE TRAGEDY. THEY ARE MY INSTRUMENTS TO LEAD YOU TO THEIR OPPOSITE. WITHOUT THEM AND WITHOUT WHAT YOU CALL SIN, HOW COULD YOU MEASURE THAT WHICH IS GOOD? THEREFORE, KNOW THIS: THERE IS NO JUDGMENT IN MY KINGDOM, FOR IF THERE WERE JUDGMENT, IT WOULD MEAN THAT I WAS DISAPPOINTED. I WHO KNOW ALL THINGS CAN NEVER BE DISAPPOINTED, BUT YOU CAN. I DO NOT GET ANGRY. YOU DO. YOU REQUIRE JUDGMENT, AND YOUR LAWS ADMINISTER IT. THAT GIVES YOU ORDER, AND THAT IS GOOD.

"BUT I AM BOTH ORDER AND CHAOS BECAUSE MY CORE IS BEYOND MEASUREMENT, AND THEREFORE BEYOND ANY ORDER YOU CAN FATHOM. THIS IS BEYOND YOUR CAPACITY TO UNDERSTAND, FOR THERE IS NO SUFFERING IN MY REALM, AND ALL THAT I CREATE, BOTH THE GOOD AND WHAT YOU CALL EVIL, FULFILLS MY ENDS. MANY OF YOUR HOLY BOOKS WARN NOT TO JUDGE LEST YOU BE JUDGED. THEY TELL YOU TO FORGIVE, FOR THAT IS DIVINE. HEED THAT.

"NOW LIFT YOUR EYES TO BEHOLD MY NEW COVENANT. THE NATIONS HAVE MISINTERPRETED THE WORD, AND EACH

CLAIMS SOLE STEWARDSHIP OF THE TRUTH. TILL NOW THERE HAS BEEN NO END TO PERSECUTION IN MY NAME. YOU SEE THAT A FATHER AND A MOTHER LOVE ALL THEIR SONS AND DAUGHTERS. ALL ARE CHOSEN. ALL ARE LOVED. THAT IS WHY I HAVE CALLED YOU HERE...TO BE WITNESS TO MY PRESENCE IN ALL PATHS AND IN ALL THINGS. I HAVE BROUGHT YOU TO THE BRINK SO YOUR APPETITE FOR PEACE AND UNITY IS GREATER THAN YOUR DESIRE FOR WAR AND SEPARATION."

Shuddering, the men gazed upward to read the still-burning creases in the stone. There were ten tablets, each with a commandment from the Voice beyond any form. Chrysallia read each one, and the Power within her interpreted. The first panel read:

I

I AM ONE. THOU SHALT PURSUE THE ONE WITHIN THEE AND WITH EACH OTHER.

Chrysallia, as the vehicle for the Word, intoned:

"I AM. I HAVE ALWAYS BEEN FROM BEFORE YOUR FIRST DAY UNTIL AFTER YOUR LAST. I AM NOT FATHER OR MOTHER. LOOK UP. YOU WILL NOT SEE A FACE OR PERSON LIKE YOURS IN MY HEAVENS, AND I AM EVEN BEYOND THAT. I HAVE MADE YOU MAN AND WOMAN BOTH INCOMPLETE FOR A PURPOSE. I HAVE MADE YOU WITHIN YOURSELVES TWO. YOU THINK AND YOU FEEL, YOU REASON AND YOU HUNGER, YOU SEEK ORDER AND CREATE NEW IDEAS. KNOW THAT YOUR PEACE BEGINS WHEN THE MAN AND WOMAN WITHIN YOU WED. YOU WILL FIND ME IN THAT PLACE. AND WHEN YOU COUPLE, THE TWO RETURN TO THE ONE, AND YOU WILL FIND ME THERE TOO. MY

NAME IS CALLED MORE OFTEN AND WITH MORE AWE WHEN UNION IS EXPERIENCED THAN IN ALL THE LITANIES IN ALL THE TEMPLES YOU HAVE ERECTED. UNITY IS THE WAY TO ME. THAT IS HOW YOU GOT THE TREASURE, FOR THAT IS THE TREASURE. THE CHEST WAS EMPTY BECAUSE THE WEALTH YOU HAVE INHERITED IS THE UNITY YOU NOW FEEL. IS THAT NOT MORE PRECIOUS THAN RICHES? ITS BOUNTY WILL BE FELT FOR EONS TO COME, FOR ALL THINGS ARE POSSIBLE WITH IT AND NOTHING WITHOUT IT. I AM ONE. YOU THE MANY COME TOGETHER TO FIND ME."

The second panel read:

II

I AM NOT A JEALOUS GOD. THOU SHALT NOT PERSECUTE IN MY NAME.

Again Chrysallia mouthed the Word:

"I HAVE MADE YOU DIFFERENT FOR A PURPOSE. IT IS EASY TO LOVE THE IMAGE STARING BACK AT YOU IN THE MIRROR. YOU CANNOT EXPERIENCE UNITY IF YOU ARE ALL ALIKE. SO I HAVE GIVEN YOU DIFFERENT LOOKS AND SHAPES, DIFFERENT HISTORIES AND DIFFERENT LANDS AND CLIMATES. DIVERSITY ABOUNDS IN MY CREATION FROM THE BEASTS OF THE PRAIRIES TO THE FISH OF THE SEA. AND TO YOU. IN EACH I HAVE INVESTED A PATH TO FIND ME AND EACH OTHER. THE MOST RIGHTEOUS AMONG YOU HAVE ALWAYS SEEN THIS. SO KNOW THAT YOU ARE ALL CHOSEN. YOU HAVE ALL BEEN GIVEN THE TRUTH, AND WHEN YOU THOUGHT DEEPLY ON IT, YOU FOUND ME HERE. NOW GO AND TEACH TOLERANCE."

The third panel read:

III

I HAVE NOT EMOTIONS. THOU SHALT NOT PORTRAY ME AS
ANGRY OR DISAPPOINTED.

From Chrysallia's lips the Voice expanded its intent:

"TELL YOUR PRIESTS I HATE NO ONE. I AM THE SOURCE OF WHAT
IS. I DO NOT HATE WHAT I CREATE. I AM NOT SURPRISED BY ANY
ACT OR OCCURRENCE. THE TRAITOR AND TYRANT ARE HERE SO
THAT YOU MAY VENERATE THE SAINT AND THE SAVIOR. AND I DO
NOT GRANT WISHES FROM PRAYER. KNOW THIS. IF YOU THINK
I ANSWERED A PRAYER IN YOUR DARKEST MOMENT, MY GIFT
WAS KNOWN BY ME BEFORE YOU ASKED IT AND THE GRANTING
WAS NOT BECAUSE I DECIDED TO CHANGE YOUR DESTINY OR
THAT OF ANY OTHER. IT WAS ALREADY ANTICIPATED IN YOUR
EXISTENCE. I CHANGE NOTHING; OTHERWISE THE UNIVERSE
WOULD BE ALTERED FROM MY DESIRED END WITH EVERY
GENUFLECTION."

The fourth panel read:

IV

THOU SHALT HONOR THY CHILDREN.

The Word passed through Chrysallia again:

"HONOR THY CHILDREN, AND THEY WILL HONOR YOU. THOSE
DEEMED THE WORST AMONG YOU HAVE BEEN ABUSED BY THEIR
PARENTS AND HAVE MADE THE WORLD PAY A PAINFUL PRICE

BECAUSE OF THAT. THE CHILD WHO IS LOVED AND TRUSTED, LOVES AND TRUSTS. FILL THEIR LIVES WITH LAUGHTER AND DO NOT FAIL TO WATCH THEM. FOR MY DEW IS STILL ON THEM IN THEIR PURITY, HONESTY, AND SPONTANEITY. THEY ARE NOT BLINDED BY THE DIFFERENCES THAT HAVE BLINDED YOU. THAT COMES FROM YOUR OWN TEACHINGS. KEEP TO YOUR ORIGINAL TRUTH AS YOU AGE AND LIVE MORE FULLY. IN THAT THE CHILD HAS INSTRUCTION FOR YOU.

The fifth panel read:

V

THOU SHALT HONOR THE WOMAN AS THOU HONOR THE MAN.

The Voice found expression again through the princess child:

"YOUR UNIVERSE FELL OUT OF ORDER WHEN YOU RESTRICTED THE WOMAN. YOU MADE HER THE SOURCE OF EVIL OR DISTRACTION IN MANY OF YOUR HOLY BOOKS. YOU FEAR HER POWER BECAUSE SHE CAN OVERCOME YOUR REASON AND STRENGTH WITH HER LOVE AND BEAUTY, WITH HER SOFTNESS. YOU DENIGRATE THINGS FEMALE, FOR YOU THINK TEARS AND COMPASSION MAKE MEN WEAK. SO YOU RULE FROM DOMINANCE AND LOGIC. YOU LET THE WOMAN WITHIN DIE TO BE A MAN WHO HIDES HIS TRUE FEELINGS AND IS NEVER KNOWN. IN THIS YOU SUFFER BECAUSE YOU CANNOT BE YOUR TRUE SELF. YOU HAVE BECOME LIKE THE MACHINES YOU HAVE CREATED. YOUR SCIENCE IS INVESTED IN POWER AND GAIN AT THE EXPENSE OF COMPASSION AND THE HEART, WHICH YOU REFUSE TO ACKNOWLEDGE. UNTIL YOU FIND THE HEART, WHICH IS UNMATCHED IN THE WOMAN, YOUR SOVEREIGNTY AND DETACHMENT WILL BRING YOU WAR, FAMINE, AND

PESTILENCE. THE WOMAN AS MOTHER AND CARETAKER WOULD NEVER ALLOW SUCH OUTCOMES. REDISCOVER HER. FIND THE HEART AND BE REDEEMED. BRING BALANCE AND HARMONY TO YOUR LIFE AND TO YOUR WORLD. IT IS IN THE WOMAN'S EMBRACE THAT YOU FIND YOUR OWN COMPLETENESS. SHE IS WHAT IS MISSING IN YOU.

The sixth panel read:

VI

THOU SHALT HONOR THE BEASTS OF THE SKY, EARTH, AND SEA.

Again Chrysallia, as the medium of the Word, intoned:

"YOU HAVE FAILED TO SEE WHY THE BEASTS OF THE EARTH ARE SACRED TO ME. YOUR ANCESTORS DID AND LIVED IN HARMONY WITH THEM. THE CREATURE IS A GIFT FOR YOU TO ELEVATE YOURSELF. THE PURITY AND GRACE OF THEM UNTOUCHED BY THINGS HUMAN BRING YOU TO MY PRESENCE, FOR IN THE COURSE OF ANIMAL EXISTENCE, YOU MOVE OUT OF YOUR TIME INTO THE REALM OF SEASONS AND MIGRATIONS, RAIN AND DROUGHT, AND IN ALL THE CREATURE SURVIVES. YOU STRUGGLE TRYING TO LIVE A MATERIAL LIFE. YOU LIE, YOU MANIPULATE, AND YOU COMPROMISE YOUR PURITY FOR GAIN OR POSITION. LOOK AT THE BEAST. IT IS ALWAYS TRUE TO ITS NATURE AND LIVES OUT ITS LIFE THROUGH THE INNER PRINCIPLE THAT DEFINES IT. THIS YOU DO NOT DO. PRESERVE THE BEAST AND FIND YOUR OWN AUTHENTICITY. LOSE THE BEAST TO YOUR OWN SELFISH EXPANSION, AND YOUR LIFE WILL BE EMPTY AND TAINTED. A VOID OF LONELINESS WILL HAUNT YOU ALL YOUR DAYS."

The seventh panel read:

VII

THOU SHALT HONOR THE EARTH IN ALL ITS FORMS.

Again the Voice spoke through Chrysallia:

"YOU HAVE PLACED ME AS A MAN IN THE SKY. THERE YOU LOOK
UP INTO THE HEAVENS AND WONDER. THERE YOU DIRECT YOUR
PRAYERS. LOOK TO THE FORESTS AND PLAINS, THE JUNGLES AND
DESERTS, THE GLACIERS AND THE SEAS. FOR I AM THERE, AND
EQUAL AWE AWAITS YOU IN THEIR EXPANSE. YOUR THEOLOGIES
HAVE MISDIRECTED YOU. THE NATIVE PEOPLES THAT LIVED IN
THESE HOLY PLACES YOU DESTROYED OR FORCED TO CONVERT
TO YOUR OWN ANSWERS. THEY HAD MORE INSTRUCTION FOR
YOU THAN YOU HAD FOR THEM. YOU DESTROY THE TREES,
POLLUTE THE WATERS, AND FOUL THE AIR. THEY DO NOT. IT
MUST ALL END NOW. PLANT, PRESERVE, AND PREVAIL. I AM THE
EARTH AS MUCH AS I AM THE SKY. I AM MOTHER AS MUCH AS I AM
FATHER. RESPECT BOTH. AND PROSPER."

The eighth panel read:

VIII

THOU SHALT CHOOSE THY PRIESTS WISELY.

Chrysallia was again the medium through which the Voice spoke:

"HE WHO TRULY REPRESENTS ME WILL NEVER LEAD YOU TO
VIOLENCE, INTOLERANCE, OR JUDGMENT. I ABIDE IN ALL.

THERE IS NO NEED TO CONVERT ANYONE UNLESS ON THEIR
OWN THEY CAN FIND ME ON YOUR PATH. ALL LEAD TO ME,
EVEN THOSE LOST, FOR IN THE END I AM INESCAPABLE. AND
YOU DO NOT HAVE TO PAY THE PRIESTS OF THE TEMPLE TO
REACH ME. LOOK WITHIN AND YOU CAN FIND ME. LOOK UP IN
THE HEAVENS. I AM WATCHING YOU. ENTER THE WILD PLACES.
I AM THERE. I LOVE THE HOLY SITES ERECTED IN MY HONOR
UNLESS THEY ARE USED TO CONDEMN OTHER HOLY PLACES
OR THE WEALTH THEY ACCUMULATE COMES OFF THE BACKS
OF THOSE THAT ARE POOR. BEAUTIFUL BUILDINGS AMIDST THE
PAIN AND NEGLECT OF THOSE WHO ARE NOT COMFORTABLE IS
NOT PLEASING TO ME. BE CAUTIOUS WHEN THOSE WHO CLAIM
TO REPRESENT ME CONTROL THE MEANING OF MY WORDS.
THEY CAN BE INTERPRETED IN MANY WAYS. WHEN YOU ARE
TOLD THERE IS ONLY ONE WAY AND ONE PATH, A WALL IS BEING
ERECTED BETWEEN YOU AND YOUR BROTHER AND YOU AND
YOUR SISTER. WHEN YOU ARE TOLD THAT YOU WILL BE SAVED
BECAUSE OF THE WORD AND OTHERS WILL NOT, YOU ARE BEING
LED ASTRAY. I AM THE AUTHOR OF LIFE AND DEATH. ALL WHO
COME INTO LIFE ARE TO MY PURPOSE AND RETURN TO ME. I
AM NOT CRUEL. I DO NOT CREATE TO PUNISH. ALL SERVE MY
PURPOSE."

The ninth panel read:

IX

THOU SHALT NOT USE MY NATURAL LAWS FOR VIOLENT ENDS

Chrysallia once more shuddered as the Voice escaped her:

"THE TIME HAS COME FOR YOU TO EXAMINE HOW THAT WHICH
YOU CALL SCIENCE IS USED. IF THERE IS NOT A MOTIVATION

FROM THE HEART FOR ITS APPLICATION, YOU ARE COURTING DISASTER. SINCE THE ANCIENT DAYS YOUR WEAPONS GET BETTER, YET EACH TIME YOU BECOME LESS SAFE. IN YOUR HOLY BOOKS YOU WERE WARNED THAT THE NEXT DESTRUCTION WILL COME THROUGH FIRE. YOU NOW HAVE THE POWER OF THE SUN IN YOUR HANDS AND IN YOUR WEAPONS. WHAT WILL YOU DO WITH IT? I SPEAK NOW TO STOP YOU. YOU HAVE USED TECHNOLOGY TO DARK ENDS AND HAVE LOST YOUR WAY IN YOUR LUST TO CONTROL AND DOMINATE YOUR BROTHER AND SISTER. I HAVE ALLOWED THAT AS I ALLOW ALL THINGS SO THAT THROUGH SUFFERING YOU SEE. REGARD YOUR OWN CREATION AND THE ANGUISH IT GENERATES EVERY DAY OF YOUR EXISTENCE. THERE YOU HAVE WAR. THERE YOU BEFOUL THE GROUND YOU WALK ON. THERE YOU HAVE PERSECUTION AND INTOLERANCE. YOUR WORLD IS COLLAPSING FROM MISUSE OF MY GIFTS. YOU HAVE MADE A GOD OF LOGIC, SO YOU CREATE WITHOUT COMPASSION. THAT IS THE PATH TO YOUR DOOM. LOSE THE HEART AND THE SOUL WILL FOLLOW. WITH THIS REVELATION YOU WILL USE MY LAWS TO UPLIFT; TO REPLENISH AND SUPPORT. A NEW WAY WILL COME WHEN YOU DESCEND MY MOUNTAIN."

The tenth panel read:

X

REMEMBER THOU KEEP HOLY EVERY DAY.

As the vessel of the Word, Chrysallia gave the final admonition:

"TO EXPERIENCE ME IN YOUR HOLY PLACES TOGETHER IS GOOD. BUT WHEN YOU LEAVE, WHAT DO YOU DO TO YOUR BROTHER AND SISTER? IT BENEFITS YOU NOT TO BE HOLY

WITHIN THE TEMPLE AND LOSE ME WHEN YOU LEAVE. YOU
ARE HOLY EVERY DAY WHEN YOU LOOK AT YOURSELF AND
SEE ME IN YOU. YOU ARE HOLY EVERY DAY WHEN YOU LOOK
AT THE STRANGER AND SEE ME LOOKING BACK AT YOU, FOR
I AM THERE. YOU ARE HOLY EVERY DAY WHEN YOU SEE THE
CREATURE ROMPING IN THE FIELDS AND SEE ME SMILING AT
YOU. THEN VIOLENCE TO THE OTHER BECOMES IMPOSSIBLE.
IT ALSO MAKES VIOLENCE TOWARD YOU IMPOSSIBLE TOO.
DO THIS AND YOU WILL ASCEND IN CONSCIOUSNESS TO THE
NEXT REVELATION, WHICH WILL COME WHEN YOU ARE
READY. YOUR RELATIONSHIP WITH ME WILL BE OF ANOTHER
LEVEL THEN, AND IT WILL BE GOOD.

"KEEP NOW THIS NEW COVENANT AS A COMPANION TO THE
OLD. BUT KNOW THIS. THESE PRECEPTS BEFORE YOU EMBRACE
ALL, OFFER YOU PEACE, AND PRESERVE THE LAND. HE WHO
CONTRADICTS THIS LEADS YOU BACK TO YOUR PERIL. GO AND
SPREAD THE WORD. PEACE UNTO YOU."

With that, the same fiery blast that cut into the stone ripped a new path down the mountain, a path they would all take together. A long silence followed. The screech of an eagle swooping toward a desert hare was heard in the distance. Chrysallia too broke the silence. Curled in a ball on the ledge where she first sat, she was weeping. Though exhausted, she felt beatified at the same time. She knew that this message came through her, a girl, and that it was a signal for a new era. The kings too were trembling, for they also felt chosen among all others to receive this Word. As they embraced, a realization set in. They were called as former enemies to give weight and substance to the message. Facing the masses united for all to see would be a miracle in itself. To then announce the new covenant would be the catalyst for the reclamation of the people and the land as well.

The kings and chieftains embraced Chrysallia and kissed her hands in obeisance. She bade them rise, for she was no more an object for idolatry than they were when they ruled supreme in their kingdoms. But the bond between them would never be broken. The pilgrimage to the mountain would be a yearly ritual. Others would be invited to follow suit so the Word could be seen by all the nations. But their journey was to be a private affair since what they embraced was directly unique to them.

The time to return to the world was at hand, but none had the energy to take the journey. They had fasted for days and were parched from the blast of the beams cutting into the mountainside. They would never make it off this sacred cliff. Part of them wished never to leave, but leave they must or the Word would die with them.

Chrysallia called them to her. She removed the Flower of Life from her sack and bade them kneel in front of it. She then poured the nectar down their burning throats, and their thirst abated. She drank herself after tending to her kings. The men were stunned. Warmth filled them as no other elixir could. Chrysallia then held the flower in front of their eyes so they could see that which refreshed them. As they contemplated its mystical beauty, a spiritual breakthrough as profound as the Word was experienced. The flower was the living symbol of the covenant in stone, for in its core were the very colors of their faces bound as one and held together by a unifying stem. Now they saw what they had heard. With that Chrysallia broke off a petal for each and fed them. Then she took for herself. They all experienced serenity unlike any other, for now the Word was in them.

But there was one more imposition that the men had to receive before their return so the new covenant could be realized. She spoke to them now in openness and trust, and they received her words as truth: "When you return to your kingdoms, select six widows who have lost children to your violence. Make them your advisors. They will ensure the outcomes that the covenant promises, and balance will be restored to the world."

The men agreed but went further. They knew the old ways of governance divided them by culture and ambition. A new order to prevent that had to be realized. They proposed that they would meet as a body every month to decide with their widowed advisors how best to apply the tenets received on this, the most sacred of days. And they agreed on a name. They would call themselves the Council for Unity. The flower would be its symbol, for it would be the stem that unified them all. The Word would have its earthly form.

Little did they know that their counterparts in Calderont had done the same thing. The old world was being shattered everywhere.

It was time to go. The men gathered at the path created for them. They took their last look at the still-burning stone that had decided their fate, and with Chrysallia leading, they descended down a new road, keeping that which was unique to each but bound by that which was common to all.

CHAPTER 16:

THE RETURN

On the way back through the desert, the men were buoyant. The stress of conflict and competition was replaced by the excitement of sharing responsibility for the world for which they were now accountable. Some recounted stories of widows who fearlessly challenged their policies for war and the fear each king felt at their rebellion. Upon returning to their realms, these women would be given roles as ministers. Others talked of projects to improve the quality of air and water. All were agreed that a plan for the planet should be fashioned with all committing resources for implementation. And the first order of business was to redirect funding for arms to a pool for the reclamation of land to ensure the vitality of the wild places. It was an exciting time. This child was indeed the Princess of Possibility, for now in their union there was little they couldn't accomplish.

But Chrysallia was more introspective. She faced a different challenge. Who knew what she would face upon returning to Calderont? It was also clear to her that the kings and chieftains had lived their lives, were married, and had children. Her life was barely beginning, and despite matters of state, she wanted these things too. Decisions would have to be made, priorities set, and action taken. Was she prepared? Would she be able to pursue a personal life? Who could she trust from her own council?

The men could verify all that they had heard and seen. She, now turning but sixteen years, was the sole witness to an experience that would be doubted by most even though her own gifts of persuasion were considerable. And then there was the matter of her dream. There was another meaning. What could that be? Would she face another trial?

The child was drained from her previous labors and, while curious, would just as soon take a very long hiatus from responsibility to digest the gravity of all her initiations. Who was she and what was she to become as a result of these preternatural passages to the headlands of Fendor?

The kings and chieftains sensed her anxiety and pledged to do what they could to help. All knew of young men who they felt would be suitable for marriage to her. But Chrysallia had no appetite to wed anyone yet fashioned by the dogmatic impositions of a still-parochial world. After her energies were tested to the limit to bring the kings and chieftains to illumination, she lacked the will to undertake a similar persuasion with young men who had their own agendas.

No, she would do better left to her own designs. What did comfort her was their pledge to convene annually and relive the expedition to Asperion. Instinctively they all turned to face her still-shimmering imprints leagues away. Even from such a great distance, the panels retained their eerie glow like some lighthouse high upon a cliff guiding sailors away from the reefs and toward safe harbor.

The time for leave-taking arrived. They had reached their initial point of embarkation, and each would take the route back to home and hearth, back to the embrace of their wives, back to the clamor of their children, and back to possibilities unthought of during their entire histories.

Chrysallia was returning to an uncertain world with a paralyzed father and an experimental council untested in decision making and with allegiances yet to be proven. Her universe, for all its promise, was in flux, and this greatly disturbed her. Yet her departure from the men whom she had come to love was a poignant one. They all knew they had been called as catalysts for monumental change, and each saw in the other the light of eternity that would be reflected by multitudes soon to be tutored to the new ways.

The men embraced and then all took the young girl to their bosoms as they would their own daughters. They loved her. She had removed the cataracts from their eyes, and what they now beheld was the gleam of the eternal in her and in them. They promised to reconvene on the Feast Day of this Revelation to renew their journey and their commitment to the precepts divinely bestowed upon them. In time entire populations would make the same journey through the desert for the same purpose. Who knows, they mused, maybe if the promise of the prophecy occurred in their lifetimes, they might yet be called to the next Revelation. With that they clasped hands, turned, and traced their way back home.

Chrysallia felt desolated. The pang of separation would remain for some time, as it always does. Even in the short visits to friends or distant family, the turning of the back in departure carries with it a wistfulness that reminds us that for all our social craving we are in many ways alone. There is awareness that in each casting off, the moment is forever lost because none of us is the same again. The child grown who departs the house for the last time, the place of beauty not to be visited again, the holidays in olden times when all was innocent of the pain to come, all conspire to make us wonder if life could ever be restored to the way it once was when the world made sense, the old were still alive, and the noise of children was the backdrop for history moving forward.

Lost for the moment in nostalgia, Chrysallia too ascended the slope to the cave leading to the crater where her flower was to be restored, and Drougen was waiting with yet another truth from the layers of symbols in her dream. Her passage through the mountain corridor was secure through the glow of her flower, and without incident she emerged to find the old man of the forest sunning himself on a rock.

She unburdened herself of all that transpired. Drougen, wizened from age, felt a joy not yet experienced, for he now knew the forests of Fendor and Maladour would be preserved. He would continue to live and feel the rapture of the deer cavorting in the sylvan dusk feeding on fallen chestnuts and savoring the delicate blooms of mountain laurel and viburnum in the hidden glades that he loved to haunt.

He greeted her warmly. "You have accomplished that which you were called to do. You, a child, have brought back harmony to our world and theirs. In the name of all that abide above and below the forested tracts, I thank you. Now the world knows the power of the flower. It seems delicate and short lived. As the days grow short, it succumbs to ice and frost and seems dead. Yet in the spring exultances it comes back to life resurrected by a loving sun calling it forth from its wintry tomb as renewed as the snake that sheds its skin. It is why we place these blooms on the tombs of our beloved departed. We are the flower. We live but a short life and also succumb. But like the flower, we will be called to new life from which there is no end to bliss. Now restore the Flower of Life to its source, for it cannot be disturbed again in your lifetime."

With that Chrysallia took the path to the altar of rock that encased the sacred flower and replaced it in its base.

She was not as sanguine as Drougen when she returned to him. The world might be restored, she thought, but she certainly was not. Her life was not in order at all. At least this is what she felt. "What of my future? What reward do I get for bringing the world of men to light?"

Drougen saw her apprehension, which would only be exacerbated by what was awaiting her. He cautioned: "There is no reward other than the fact that you were a participant in the ongoing evolution of the world. Delight in what you have saved and delight in what you have created. You are the most fortunate of children. They will sing of you long after you are in another form. Mothers will name their daughters after you. Fathers will dream bigger dreams for their daughters too because of what you have done. That is your legacy. Your father helped children to face their dragons. You will teach them that they can affect history armed with the truth of a simple flower."

Chrysallia was mollified by Drougen's good counsel to her, but she was still apprehensive. There was a sense of disturbance gnawing within even in this most idyllic place. She thought it was the missing piece to her dream. But it wasn't. She pressed Drougen to fulfill his promise: "What is the other meaning to my dream so that I may return home purged of any doubt about my destiny?"

Drougen bade her sit, and he kept his promise: "Your destiny, my child, will take many turns, and you know enough not to fear any outcome. What will unfold cannot be altered, so put yourself in the stream as I instructed you and do not resist what awaits. This was the first message of your vision. You cannot escape the inevitable. But there is a richer meaning as well.

"Now that you have passed your trial, it will be revealed to you. Part of the dream vision warned you of a death to come. And indeed that was so. The gate to the fountain separated the eight boys from the world on the other side, a world they were not suited to enter. As you crossed unobstructed, it signaled that you indeed were ready. A child could not reclaim the world, but a young girl could. The signs were there before your reverie. You left home. You crossed a threshold. You faced your dark side and controlled your appetites. These are the prerequisites for a heroic life, an authentic life.

"But now there is another message that will signal your departure from the innocence you still enjoy. The male voice of Viladon had another function in forecasting the death of your childhood. All girls lose their innocence through men. In their embrace the girl dies and the woman is born. The tree is a symbol of that manhood, and in your girlish fear of the unknown you felt terror and fled it. When you arrived at the gate, your fascination for the young men and women in all manner of embrace stirred that which was ready to be manifested in you as well. This grew in intensity when you encountered the statues and later the boy by the lake.

"The time was not right for you then because discipline, not distraction, was required of you given the enormity of your mission. But the inner voice left you a compelling message that the end of that childhood is not to be feared but enjoyed. And the truth of that is how the dream ends. You not only returned to the thing you feared, but you ascended it in triumph. You were the conqueror, not the tree. It is the sign of the power of the woman whose beauty and allure will conquer the strongest of men. That is why men fear, for they are without defense. Use your gift wisely, and they will elevate you. Abuse it, and their fears minimize you both. So, my child, in your return a new life awaits you."

Chrysallia thought of the boy at the lake, and the fire within her returned. Nothing could hinder her now, she thought, for she had fulfilled her calling. What obligation could impede her?

Drougen, however, was not through. "There is another message underneath this one that is equally true and will be of equal benefit to you. It has to do with the tree. In many beliefs the tree is the center of the universe. It has been called by many names, but it is most associated with good and evil and life and death. It has a duality that we find compelling. It represents us; that is why the tree must always be revered."

Chrysallia loved trees. They were sacred in Calderont and were rarely felled. But she never saw them as symbols of things human. "How can the tree be a symbol of a human being?" she queried.

Drougen provided her answer: "The tree is like us in this sense. Its limbs seek the sun and sky. In this aspect it is a force that seeks the light just as a part of us does. But it moves in another direction equally profound. Its roots seek the world unseen, the world of mystery, the world we fear. The darkness is the womb and tomb of the earth. And we are just as much a part of that as the realm of light.

"The tree reminds us that we are anchored in the earth and all its instinctive energy and mystery while at the same time we seek the heavens and the light that brings order to our waking world. We must be both, for a tree without roots will surely fall as quickly as a man who will not acknowledge the unseen force that is within him. He will break when his reason or senses fail him, for he is a stranger to his inner life, which is eternal. So, my dear Princess, the tree is your compass and reminder to live in harmony with all your energies, both the light and the dark. To not do so is to see a devil around every corner and live a life punctuated by fear, stress, and isolation."

Chrysallia bowed to the all-wise Drougen. Now she could see that he truly was the old man in her dream walking toward the tree and sadly realizing that she must undergo great tribulation to know what he now knew. This she had done in crossing the thresholds into her uncharted realms both physically and within. She was now ready to face that last unknown confronting her on the road to Calderont. And she would need all her strength and more.

For in that moment her father died and the Terruleans hiding in the forest invaded Calderont.

Unaware of the conflagration awaiting her, she took her leave of Drougen and turned to face the darkness once again. Before she knew it, the old man was gone. She would have to pass through the mountain corridor one last time without light. Steeling herself, she prayed for strength. A plaintive sound escaped the mouth of a solitary child carrying both the knowledge and weight of the world at the same time. "Mother," she cried.

The sound of the word ripped through her. "Mother," the guiding light of her youth, gone with barely time to mourn. "Mother," she cried again as a lost cub bleats for comfort far from its den.

The tears she had stored to protect her father's grief and the people's anxiety finally found its release, and she wept bitterly. Like her father she was robbed of love when she needed it most. Again the word stored away in protection for the disturbance it would have caused during her quest finally found its expression: "Mother." The anguish of her cry filled the crater and reverberated back as if the mountain itself joined in chorus for her loss.

As she lifted her head at the echo of her lamentation, there was movement in the undergrowth. Her eyes could not see through the teary film, but she heard the rustling. In a moment of unwarranted hope, the word escaped her one more time. "Mother?"

There in the thick bush was Salasar. In a pounce she was on her. Chrysallia hurled herself at the cat's neck in embrace, and as their eyes met the cat held her glance and said, "YES."

The End

Made in the USA
Lexington, KY
09 July 2014